"I don't want you to be

"I'll do everything I can to protect you."

"What can I do for you?" Meg asked. "I want to do something too."

"You can love me," Nick said.

Meg laughed. "That's too easy," she said. "I do that already."

Then Nick smiled, and Meg realized all those wonderful flirty words were true, that everything they'd both been saying, they'd meant. She looked then, really hard, at Nick, tried to see who it was she felt so instantly connected to, tried to understand what it was about him that made her feel more eager to live than she'd ever dreamed. But all she could see was he loved her, and for the moment, that was all she needed to see . . .

Also available in *The Sebastian Sisters* series by Susan Beth Pfeffer, published by Bantam Books:

EVVIE AT SIXTEEN
THEA AT SIXTEEN
CLAIRE AT SIXTEEN
SYBIL AT SIXTEEN

MEG AT SIXTEEN

THE SEBASTIAN SISTERS

SUSAN BETH PFEFFER

BANTAM BOOKS

TORONTO · NEW YORK · LONDON · SYDNEY · AUCKLAND

THE SEBASTIAN SISTERS: MEG AT SIXTEEN

A BANTAM BOOK 0 552 40149 1

First published in USA by Bantam Books, a division of Bantam Doubleday Dell Publishing Group, Inc.

First publication in Great Britain

PRINTING HISTORY
Bantam edition published 1991

Bantam Books are published by Transworld Publishers Ltd., 61–63 Uxbridge Road, Ealing, London W5 5SA, in Australia by Transworld Publishers (Australia) Pty. Ltd., 15–23 Helles Avenue, Moorebank, NSW 2170, and in New Zealand by Transworld Publishers (N.Z.) Ltd., Cnr. Moselle and Waipareira Avenues, Henderson, Auckland.

Made and printed in Great Britain by
BPCC Hazell Books
Aylesbury, Bucks, England
Member of BPCC Ltd.

MEG AT SIXTEEN

CHAPTER ONE

"What a dump!"

"I know," Sybil Sebastian said. "But I only got home yesterday. I haven't had a chance to unpack yet."

Claire Sebastian laughed. "Home," she said. "You're the only one of us who feels comfortable calling this dive a home."

"I call it home too," Thea Sebastian said. "Maybe not the home of my dreams, but home."

"It's the home of my dreams," Sybil declared. "And I'll thank all of you to treat it with respect."

Evvie Sebastian Steinmetz Greene smiled. "Fear and loathing is more like it," she replied. "It's been what, five years since Aunt Grace died and sort of left us this place, and I still expect to see her every time I walk through the door."

"Her memory does linger," Thea agreed, wrinkling her nose. "Sort of like moldy cheese."

"You never gave her a chance," Claire said. "Sure, on

the outside, she was cold and cruel, but inside, she was miserable and rotten. I always liked that about her."

"Five years," Thea said. "Do you remember that first awful Christmas here?"

"Let's not remember the awful times," Sybil said. "There were too many of them that year."

The sisters were silent for a moment, thinking of all that had happened five years before, the move to Boston, the big fight between Evvie and their father, Nick, and then Nick's death.

"He would have been so proud of you," Evvie said to Sybil, and they all knew whom she was talking about. "Graduating with honors from Princeton."

"I liked it there," Sybil said. "But I was always glad to come back here for vacations."

Evvie laughed. "Thank goodness for Aunt Grace's nasty will," she declared. "Leaving the house in trust until the birth of her first legitimate Christian grandson."

"Speaking of which," Claire said. "When are your legitimate Jewish sons arriving? I want to play aunty."

"Sam's bringing them in a couple of hours," Evvie replied. "If you thought they were monsters before, wait until you see them now. They're both crawling and they have this terrible tendency to bump into each other. Sam keeps trying to point them in opposite directions, but that means twice as much chasing for us. I think twins were Grace's curse on me."

"I can't wait to have children," Thea declared. "Of course medical school came first, and then meeting the right man, which I don't seem to have done quite yet, but I really want a large family."

"You want it all," Evvie said. "You always did."

Thea smiled. "I did, didn't I," she said. "I just never thought of it that way."

"You have it all," Claire pointed out to Evvie. "A husband, children, and a career. Almost a Ph.D. What a lousy example you've set for all of us."

"Sure," Evvie said. "And that's exactly the life you've made for yourself, Claire. Domesticity. Education."

"I took some classes once," Claire replied. "No, that isn't even true. I tried three times to take classes, but all three times, something came up right around the second or third session. Shoots in London. Vacations on the Riviera. What's a girl to do?"

"Keep looking beautiful," Thea said. "You're on the Riviera beaches while I'm memorizing bones."

"That's the difference between bones and bone structure," Claire said. "I knew from birth high cheekbones were my way out of this madness."

Sybil tossed some clothing off her bed and stretched out. "What about Schyler?" she asked. "Any change in that relationship?"

"Schyler wants to marry me," Claire said. "And I'm not opposed. I am twenty-three, after all, and it's about time I made my first marriage."

"Are you going to marry him?" Thea asked. "Two weddings this summer? Can I stand it?"

Claire shrugged, and the sisters smiled at the familiarity of the gesture. "I keep telling him he just isn't rich enough," she replied. "I know he's gorgeous, and he's doing well enough, but shouldn't my first husband be somebody just terribly rich? Then after that doesn't work out, I can marry for love."

"Do you love him?" Thea asked.

"I don't know," Claire said. "You're the love expert around here. You tell me."

"Evvie's the expert," Sybil said. "I wish I could have been at your anniversary party."

"Five years," Evvie said. "It feels longer somehow."

"It is longer," Claire said. "You and Sam have been together what, ten, eleven years?"

"Something like that," Evvie replied. "It's gotten so I can't remember a time without him. It was a funny kind of a party, Syb, with none of you there."

"I'm sorry," Thea said. "Interns cannot call their lives their own. You wouldn't believe the maneuvering it took to get this weekend off."

"They insisted on a screen test," Claire said. "I begged them. I said, 'My oldest sister is celebrating her fifth anniversary and she's married to the last decent man in America,' and they said, 'Shut up and act.' As though I knew how."

"Have you heard anything yet?" Sybil asked. "I can't imagine you a movie star."

"Oh I can," Thea said. "Claire was born to be one."

"I, of course, agree," Claire said, but then she giggled. "That's a first. My agreeing with Thea. My agent's optimistic, but that's the nature of agents. I don't care. If the movie comes through, great. If it doesn't, I still have a lot of good years of modeling left, and there's always Schyler, and what's his name. Donald. He asked me to marry him a couple of days ago, and I said I'd see if the wedding this weekend put me in a romantic enough mood. Of course if it does, I'll still never marry him. Donald's certainly rich enough, but that's where his charms begin and end."

"You wouldn't marry him just for his money," Thea said.

"Well, on second thought, why not?" Claire asked. "Isn't that what Megs is about to do?"

"Claire!" Evvie said sharply. "That's not true."

"You're not about to tell me it's love," Claire said. "Not after Nicky."

"There are different kinds of love," Evvie replied. "Besides, you of all people wouldn't want Megs to fall in love like she did with Nicky. All that grand passion you kept mocking."

"I had my doubts too," Sybil said. "When Megs first told us. But I think she's going to be very happy. She loved being married, you know. She loved all that domesticity."

"She's loved her job too," Evvie said. "I've never been so proud of her as when she went back to school and got a degree in physical therapy. And I've lived close enough to her to see the difference it's made in her. She's more self-confident. She's proud of herself for the first time. She was always proud of us, and of Nicky too, rightly or wrongly, but the past couple of years have been different. Her face gets that glow when she talks about her work, and how well she does it."

"So what are you saying?" Claire asked. "Are you happy or not happy with this marriage?"

Evvie took a deep breath. "I can't really say," she replied. "I know it's been five years, but there's a part of me that still hasn't accepted Nicky's death. Maybe because the end was so ugly. I don't know. Things aren't resolved for me yet, but at least I'm in therapy where my doctor and I work on it. I alternate between guilt and anger. That isn't even true. Sometimes there is so much longing for him. When Rob and Mickey were born, I wanted him there. I wanted him to see his grandsons. Mick looks like him. You can see the Prescott side in him."

"Then Nicky would have favored Robby," Claire said. "That was the way he operated."

"Old resentments die hard," Thea declared.

"Yes they do," Claire said.

"We all had a different Nicky," Sybil said. "I thought about that a lot, especially the last couple of years. Megs was pretty much the same for all of us, even you, Claire. But Nicky was a different person for each one of us. Maybe because we each had our best view of him at different spots in his life. Not ours, but his. I never knew him as well as I did the day he died, and you didn't really know him at all then, Evvie."

"I didn't know anything or anyone then," Evvie replied. "I was so confused about so many things."

"I knew Nicky," Thea said. "He never changed for me."

"That's what I mean," Sybil replied. "Nicky changed enormously after my accident. We all did, but Nicky changed the most. It isn't that I knew him the best, that I had the single best view of him. Just that the Nicky I knew was the one who was changed by my accident, and the Nicky you knew was the romantic, and the Nicky Claire knew, well, I shudder to think about that one, and the Nicky Evvie knew was the ambitious and loving family man. Do you know what I mean? Am I making sense?"

Claire nodded. "You're making sense," she declared. "After all, Megs knew a completely different Nicky. She fell in love with him when she was sixteen, and no matter what happened, that was the Nicky she knew."

"It isn't like that with Sam and me," Evvie said. "We grow, we change. We just do it together."

"You and Sam aren't Nicky and Megs," Sybil replied. "The only thing you have in common is that you fell in love at sixteen."

"That's not the only thing," Evvie said. "But I guess the differences are more relevant than the similarities."

"You even sound like a psychologist," Claire said.

"Have you been in therapy?" Thea asked.

"*Moi*?" Claire replied, raising her eyebrows in mock horror. "Perfect me?"

"What's the matter?" Thea asked. "Afraid it would lower your cheekbones?"

Claire shook her head. "There was a moment," she said. "Right after that ridiculous elopement business. We were back in Missouri, Megs and I, while Nicky was staying on in Portland with you, Sybs, and I was feeling really very wounded. Megs wouldn't talk to me about what I'd done, and frankly, I wanted some kind of reaction from her. Approval, rage, I almost didn't care, just as long as she would acknowledge it. Which, of course, she couldn't, because to acknowledge it would be to acknowledge that I was stronger than Nicky, that I had taken on his responsibilities."

"It wasn't that simple," Evvie said.

"Maybe not," Claire replied. "But it seemed that way to me. So I was hurting. And I was feeling bad about the elopement itself, what I'd done to Scotty, what he'd done to me for that matter. I was only sixteen. At the time I felt like I was thirty. Nicky knew that. He even told me how young I was, but I didn't believe him. Look what I'd just pulled off. Getting all that money from his father."

"What's the point?" Thea asked. "Well, I'm sorry, but it's not my favorite topic, that elopement. I was involved too, you know. I was used."

"You weren't even there," Claire pointed out. "You had to be told about it."

"Exactly," Thea said. "I had to be. Do you think Scotty would have gone along with your grand scheme if he hadn't been in love with me?"

"It was seven years ago," Sybil said. "Do we have to fight about it today?"

"I'm sorry," Thea said, and she managed a smile. "Some battle wounds don't heal."

"I think that's my point," Claire said. "You were the one who asked me about therapy, after all."

"I'm sorry I ever did," Thea said. "Can we change the subject now?"

"No," Evvie said. "Let Claire finish. Neither one of you has ever been any good at that, letting the other one finish."

Claire shrugged. "It isn't important," she said. "Just that I decided then I could either be whiny and miserable like Thea, or I could accept who I was and what my life had been and go on from there. Which I did. So no, I'm not in therapy, never have been, never will be. No insult intended, Evvie, I'm sure you'll be brilliant at it."

"I'm not so sure," Evvie said. "But I'll give it my best shot."

Sybil looked at her sisters and laughed. "Why is it we love each other so much and whenever we get together, we want to kill each other?"

"That isn't true," Thea said. "Sure, Claire and I have

our moments, but otherwise we all get along just fine."

"I seem to remember a certain moment at my graduation," Sybil said. "Just six weeks ago. A battle royal between you and Evvie."

"The twins were too young to be weaned," Thea said. "That's all. I am going to be a pediatrician, after all. I would have thought Evvie would be happy to benefit from my experiences."

"You experience nursing twins and working on your thesis simultaneously," Evvie said. "Then come back to me with your profound advice."

"They're going at it again," Claire said. "Good move, Sybil."

"I was just making a point," Sybil said. "Not trying to start World War Three."

"I'm sorry," Thea said. "It's this damn wedding."

"Ah," Claire said. "The truth comes out."

"Will you listen for just once," Thea said. "I know I should be happy for Megs, getting married again. But inside of me, there's a part that's just dying. It's been like that since she told us, which, if you remember correctly, was at Sybil's graduation. That was when I started picking fights with all of you. And that was when you were all more than willing to fight right back."

Evvie nodded. "He's a good man," she said. "And it's obvious how much he loves her."

"But does she love him?" Claire asked.

"Does it matter?" Evvie asked.

"Of course it does," Thea said. "Megs is still a young woman. She shouldn't settle, the way Claire seems to be willing to."

"Potshot, Thea," Claire said. "Not really called for."

Thea ignored her. "I want to be happy for Megs," she

said. "The wedding's tomorrow, for God's sake. It's just, do you remember that night when Clark brought over the videotape?"

"Thea," Claire said. "Drop it."

"I can't," Thea replied. "I think about it a lot. How many people get to see the moment when their parents met? The moment when they fell in love."

"They didn't fall in love just at that instant," Claire said.

"They didn't?" Thea said. "Then you didn't see the same videotape I did."

"They did," Sybil said. "I know they did, and what's more important, they know they did. But what difference does that make? You can't possibly want Megs to stop her life at that moment, Thea. Of all of us, you know the most about loss and the need to go on."

Claire smiled. Thea didn't seem to notice.

"We all want Megs to be happy," Evvie declared. "We just have different images of how that should be."

"Do you like the idea of this marriage?" Thea asked her. "Honestly now."

"Honestly, I don't know," Evvie replied. "Sometimes I'm very happy for her. Sometimes I think about Nicky, and I know it's ridiculous, but I feel like she's betraying him. If their love was so perfect then how can she be marrying someone else?"

"Would you ever remarry, if Sam died?" Sybil asked.

"I can't even think about that," Evvie said. "It panics me. Isn't that ridiculous? Levelheaded Evvie, in a state of total terror."

"I'm happy for her," Sybil said. "I think it's really nice she's getting married."

"You have a vested interest," Thea declared. "Megs

moves out of this house, and you move right in. Your very own Beacon Hill mansion. At least until there's a legitimate Christian grandson."

"That's not fair," Claire said. "This house is available to all of us. Sybil's just going to be going to graduate school here, that's all."

"That isn't all, and we all know it," Thea said. "We know what Sybil was willing to do to keep this house."

"My," Claire said. "We are in an ugly mood today."

"We have our share of ugly truths," Thea said.

"She was sixteen," Claire said. "Just. And you know the kind of pressure Nicky could assert. Besides, whatever happened was between Sybil and Evvie and Sam, and if they can all handle it, I don't see why it should bother you."

"I hate this house," Evvie said. "Megs offered it to Sam and me when I was expecting, and I'm so glad I turned her down. It does ugly things to us to be here. Sybil may think of it as home and she's welcome to it as far as I'm concerned, but it's a cruel house, and it makes us all say and think cruel things."

Thea started to cry. "I'm sorry," she said. "Sybil, I know it wasn't your fault. It's just I associate that business, your birthday, all of it, with Nicky's dying, and now Megs is getting remarried, and somehow that makes it feel like Nicky really is dead. Is that dumb? It's been five years, but I still have dreams that he's alive, that it's all been a scheme of his, and he and Megs are just waiting, the way they waited all those years ago, when Aunt Grace wouldn't let them get married. It's like when Megs gets married tomorrow, we're really burying Nicky, and that hurts so much."

"I didn't believe he was dead until we scattered the

ashes," Claire said. "When was that, a year after he died? Scattering them in the ocean at Eastgate. I could feel him then, so intensely, what he was and what he wanted to be, and then for the first time ever I guess, I felt at peace about him, and I felt he was at peace too. I know you think I didn't love Nicky, but in some ways I loved him more than any of you." She paused for a moment. "And in some ways, not," she declared. "No point getting too maudlin."

"I wish Megs would come downstairs already," Evvie said. "Clark is coming over in an hour or so, and we have a lot of things to do this evening."

"Let her stay up there as long as she wants," Thea said. "The longer she stays there the less it feels like she's getting married tomorrow."

"She needs the time alone," Sybil said. "She's burying a few of her own ghosts this afternoon."

The sisters were silent for a moment, then Thea changed the subject.

"Do you really think you'll be happy here?" she asked Sybil. "Megs can rent out the house, you know, and you could get an apartment, or live in university housing. You don't have to stay here, if you don't want to."

"I want to," Sybil said. "I've wanted to since the moment we first moved here. Evvie may hate this house, but it's where I feel strongest. It's funny. I even walk better here."

"It's all yours, as far as I'm concerned," Claire said. "I promise if I marry Schyler or what's his name, Donald, I won't reproduce."

"I wish I had time to," Thea said. "I wish I had time to sneeze. They run you ragged when you're an intern."

"And you love it," Evvie said. "Admit it, Thea."

"I love it," Thea said. "And I love all of you, my lousy mood notwithstanding. I even love Clark. What's he going to think if the bride to be is hiding in the attic reading old love letters when he comes in?"

"I doubt he'll be surprised," Evvie said. "Clark doesn't have any illusions."

"Clark is nothing but illusions," Sybil said. "He even thinks we're wonderful."

Claire laughed.

"You too," Sybil said. "He had your first *Vogue* cover framed, and gave it to Megs. I thought that was a wonderful thing for him to do."

"I'll be nice to the old goat today, I promise," Claire said. "Sybil, you absolutely have to straighten out this room. I cannot bear to see such chaos."

"Help me, then," Sybil said.

"We all will," Evvie said. "Come on, Thea. Let's show some family unity here."

Thea nodded. "Family unity," she said. "I like the sound of that."

The sisters threw Sybil's things around, trying to make some order out of the mess. They worked mostly in silence, and could hear the sounds of their mother in the attic, moving boxes, pausing to examine things.

"Margaret Winslow Sebastian," Evvie said suddenly. "I guess today she's putting that name to rest as well."

CHAPTER TWO

"What a dump," Margaret Winslow whispered, and then, as she was in the habit of doing at her aunt Grace's home, she looked around to confirm no one had heard her.

Not that there were spies listening to her every word. Far from it. As far as Meg could see, no one cared a whit what she said, or why she said it. But there was so much Aunt Grace disapproved of, and calling perfectly lovely places dumps would probably rank high on her list.

Meg examined her bedroom at Aunt Grace's summer cottage in Eastgate. It was, she knew, a perfect room. One window overlooked the gardens, the other window showed the ocean. Aunt Grace had had the room redecorated three years ago when Meg had officially moved in with her, and given Aunt Grace's rather peculiar attitudes toward what young girls liked, she had done a fine job. Or the decorator had, and Aunt Grace hadn't cared enough to argue. The walls were powder-blue, the woodwork a gleaming white, and there was even a canopy bed. The first time Meg had seen that bed, she'd burst into tears, and that had precipitated one of those dreaded confrontations between her and her aunt.

"What's wrong with it?" Aunt Grace had demanded, not unreasonably, Meg knew then and now.

"It reminds me of the one I used to have," Meg wept.

That turned out not to be an adequate enough reason to get rid of it, so the canopy, and for that matter, Meg, remained. In three years' time, Meg had learned to like the bed. She liked the room too, she supposed, at least as much as any other room she'd stayed in since her parents' deaths.

Meg sighed deeply, and looked through the window toward the ocean. It was her sixteenth birthday, and she knew she shouldn't be spending it thinking about her parents. There was no point thinking about them anyway; dead was dead and they would never come back and rescue her. The thought made her smile. Before her parents had died, her favorite book had been *A Little Princess*. In there, the orphan truly needed rescuing. Only by Meg's own lonely standards, could she claim to be so burdened.

Birthdays, Meg realized suddenly, were the worst, the absolute worst. She'd been unhappy the entire week, without being able to figure out why, and now the truth was staring right at her. She hated her birthday. When her parents were alive, her birthdays were splendid, filled with festivities, and presents, and sweets. There were at least twenty children at her party, and for weeks, she and her mother would conspire about all the details, going shopping for new dresses for both of them, having endless discussions with the cook about just how the birthday cake should be decorated, debating which lucky children should be invited, and which should be left out. Her birthday plans had been fun, and the days themselves were never anticlimactic. She could still remember the morning she woke up to find the four-foot-high dollhouse in her bedroom, with real electricity, and the most cunning furniture: a Queen Anne style dining room, and a perfect Victorian parlor, which, now that she thought about it, bore a strong resemblance to Aunt Grace's Beacon Hill parlor. Had the furniture been commissioned to match? She would never know, since with her parents' deaths, the dollhouse, like so much else of their lives, vanished, sold or put away in storage, or given to some cousin or other, to help pay off her father's debts. Not for the first time, Meg was uncomfortably aware of how similar the words *death* and *debt* were.

But that dollhouse! It had simply materialized in her room that day. She woke up to find it there. How had her parents managed that? It seemed magical to her then, and now as well, now that she lived with Aunt Grace, whose every footstep seemed to thunder through the houses she owned.

Meg turned away from the ocean and tried to remind herself how fortunate she was. When her parents had died, she'd been left with nothing. Her parents, Aunt Grace had explained to Meg on more than one occasion, thought the sole function of money was to spend it. Meg couldn't see what else one was supposed to do with it, but she was always too frightened to challenge Aunt Grace on that, or any other subject. What few assets did remain, though, Aunt Grace, and Uncle Marcus, Aunt Grace's younger brother, managed to save and invest, and turn into what was always referred to as a "small" trust fund for Meg.

How small Meg was never sure, but she assumed it was very small indeed.

"You are fortunate you have family to provide for you," Aunt Grace had declared at the funeral. That was the only real memory Meg had of the funeral, that, and the strange feeling she had because such an important dress had been bought for her without the help of her mother. It couldn't have been easy to find a black dress for an eleven-year-old. It was velvet, Meg remembered, and hot in the early-fall weather. It had a white lace collar, but so many ladies had bent down to kiss her that the collar ended up permanently stained with lipstick and powder, and the dress had been given to the poor. They were welcome to it.

Meg tried to remember if her eleventh birthday had been her most perfect one, but it didn't seem any better than any of the others she could remember. The dress, the cake, the party, the gifts, nothing stood out at the time or now. A week later, she and her parents had taken the *Queen Mary* to England, and spent the summer traveling around Europe. She remembered Switzerland the most fondly, but she'd always loved Switzerland. They'd spent a winter there, when she was younger, and it was a magical country. Meg had flown home alone, to start the school year at Miss Arnold's School, which she had begun attending the year before, and her parents had flown to Kenya for a safari. It was in Kenya that their plane had crashed, a small chartered airplane, whose pilot had made a fatal miscalculation. The communication system was so primitive that Meg's parents had been dead for almost a week before anybody knew. Their bodies, Uncle Marcus had explained to her, had been destroyed so badly that cremation was the only proper thing to do. Meg supposed the bodies had burned, but possibly the heat had swollen them, or animals had eaten them. No one told her, and the choice of nightmares kept her awake for many, many nights thereafter.

So the funeral had been closed casket, and almost two weeks after the actual deaths, and someone had bought a black velvet dress for her to wear. "Miss Arnold wishes to see you. There's been some bad news." The memories were all a jumble, and in her dreams, Miss Arnold frequently turned into a lion or a hyena, who threatened to eat her while Meg's parents stood by helplessly. Of course, Miss Arnold had actually been very nice about it, and had attended the funeral, and seen to it that all the girls at her school treated Meg kindly for the first few days. After that, Meg no longer cared how she was treated. Not that anyone was cruel. No one was ever cruel to her, not even Uncle Marcus's endless noisy children, with whom Meg was forced to spend that Christmas. Sometimes they'd even stop playing when she entered the room, as though games were an affront to her mourning. They weren't cruel to her that summer either, or the following Christmas, or even that following summer, so no one was able to understand, not even Meg, why on her thirteenth birthday she'd gone swimming in the ocean, well after everyone else had gone to bed, and swum so far out that her obvious intention was never to swim back. Only the good fortune of a pair of young lovers on the beach, seeing what she was doing and having the strength to swim out after her and pull her back to shore, had kept her from drowning. Meg's life was filled with good fortune.

"I wash my hands of her!" Uncle Marcus had declared, and there was only Aunt Grace left to take her in. Meg's mother had been an only child, and her parents had died within a year of their daughter's accident. So Aunt Grace had the bedroom at Eastgate redecorated with a canopy bed, and Meg had moved in.

It wasn't so bad, she knew. Her school year she continued to spend at Miss Arnold's, and Thanksgiving, Christmas, and Easter were spent in Beacon Hill. Summers at Eastgate were all right, even with Aunt Grace's many restrictions. Not too much sun. No unsupervised swimming (well, she'd brought that one on herself). No socializing with the year-rounders (but then, none of them were supposed to do that, including Isabelle Sinclair, who was madly in love with the grocery bag boy). No excursions without Aunt Grace's explicit permission. No fun, really, but then Meg wasn't sure she remembered what fun was anymore. She supposed she must occasionally have fun at Miss Arnold's, all the other girls did, and they didn't shun her, as they did some of the more studious, less entertaining girls. She knew she had gone from Poor Meg to Meg at some point during her years there, but she couldn't spot the exact moment, and she couldn't recall ever really enjoying herself. But that didn't matter. Nothing mattered.

I'm sixteen, Meg thought. Today I am sixteen. In two more years, I'll be finished with high school, and I'll make my debut. All her friends were already discussing what they would wear at their coming-out parties. Meg hoped Aunt Grace wouldn't be offended if she got one of her friends' mothers to help her with the gown. Aunt Grace had the most abominable taste in clothes. Not her own, which were tweedy in the wintertime, and floral in the summer, but in the ones she selected for her niece.

Meg tried to imagine herself in her first formal evening gown. She knew she'd be pretty; everyone always said she was, and that wasn't the sort of thing people lied about. Boys would dance with her all night long. It wouldn't matter that all she had left to her was a small trust fund. She was Grace Winslow's ward, and Grace was a wealthy woman. That made Meg an heiress, as Aunt Grace was fond of pointing out to her. "You can never be too careful about the boys you get to know. Some of them can smell money a mile away. They'll pretend to be in love with you, only because of your relationship with me, and then they'll steal your money and break your heart. You must only see suitable young men, young men who come from your own world. No one else can be trusted." That speech, Meg knew, was the equivalent for Aunt Grace of the birds and the bees.

Only suitable boys, then, would be asked to her coming-out party, and Meg supposed that a year or two after, she would marry one of them. She didn't know which one yet, or care. Maybe she'd met him, maybe she hadn't. She'd go to college for a year or so, then announce her engagement, and get married, probably by the time she was twenty. Being married had to be better than living with Aunt Grace.

Meg hated herself when she felt like that, disloyal to the only member of her family who was willing to put up with her. She knew she should love Aunt Grace, or at least be grateful to her, or at the very least respect her, but mostly all she could manage was dread. Just being in the same room with her frequently made Meg shiver. And when Aunt Grace turned her full focus of attention on her, Meg didn't know how she survived.

"What a dump," she whispered again. It was a catchphrase she used to give herself strength. Bitsy Marshall had taught it to her. Bitsy's mother said it all the time. Bitsy's mother went to the movies, and could do imitations of all the stars, but her best was her Bette Davis, and Bette Davis had said "What a dump" in some movie or another, so Bitsy's mother said it, and Bitsy said it, and Meg said it too, when no one was listening. It wasn't as though she could do a Bette Davis imitation, so she didn't try. She just said it, mostly to herself, but sometimes under her breath. "What a dump." It kept her going, that phrase. She frequently felt grateful to Bette Davis for ever having said it.

There was a knock on the door. Meg flushed with guilt. Had someone heard her saying it, and did they think she was complaining about her room? "I will not tolerate whining and complaints," Aunt Grace had said to her shortly after she'd moved in. "You are a most fortunate child, and you should appreciate all the kindness you've been shown."

"Come in," Meg said, hoping her voice hadn't cracked with terror. Aunt Grace didn't like that either.

Aunt Grace walked in. "Your dress has arrived," she declared. "I thought I would bring it to you myself. Happy birthday, Margaret."

"Thank you," Meg said. She'd risen from her chair as soon as Aunt Grace had walked in, and now, she knew, she was expected to walk over to her aunt and give her a kiss, as well as take the box from her. She willed herself into action. Aunt Grace's skin was as soft as her face was hawklike. Meg brushed her lips against her aunt's cheek in what passed as a gesture of affection in that household.

"I trust you'll like the dress," Aunt Grace said.

"I'm sure I will, Aunt Grace," Meg said.

"What's that you said?" Aunt Grace asked. "You

must learn to speak up, Margaret. This mumbling of yours is a disgusting habit."

"I'm sorry," Meg said. She didn't think she mumbled, although it was true she spoke softly, and many people had to ask her to repeat what she'd said. It surprised her that anybody cared enough to want to hear. She would have to learn to speak louder, she supposed. "I said I was sure I would like the dress, Aunt Grace." Lies had to be spoken loudest of all.

"Your guests will be arriving shortly," Aunt Grace said. "Have you bathed?"

Meg nodded. "I'm all ready, except for the dress," she said.

"Very well," Aunt Grace said, and then she cleared her throat. Meg immediately tensed up. "You are sixteen now, Margaret. I suppose a mother's duty on her daughter's sixteenth birthday is to discuss with her some of life's harsher truths."

There had been no harsh truths in her mother's heart, Meg knew. And Aunt Grace wasn't her mother. She felt herself getting faint with resentment.

"When a girl is sixteen, she is physically capable of bearing children," Aunt Grace declared. "Her body is eager for that sort of animal labor, so her emotions turn to boys, who can give her their seed. She mistakes those feelings for love."

Meg nodded. It was the only action she was capable of.

"Boys will of course take advantage of this confusion," Aunt Grace continued. "The male of the species enjoys nothing more than taking advantage of a female's need to reproduce. They whisper words of love that the female wants to hear, promise her a future together, and then they have their way with her. Do you know what having their way actually means, Margaret?"

"I think so," Meg said. It seemed the safest response.

"In any decent society, a girl's reputation is paramount," Aunt Grace said. "A girl who allows a boy to have his way with her is thought of as cheap. Such a girl never makes a good marriage, but goes on to a life of sin and degradation. True, she may marry, but if she does, it will be to a man of a lower social order, one who will not treat her with respect, and indeed, she doesn't deserve that respect. No girl who goes to her marriage bed impure deserves the respect of her husband. Virginity is the one true gift a bride can offer her groom. Am I making myself clear?"

"Yes, Aunt Grace," Meg said.

"Very well," Aunt Grace declared. "I know your parents would have wanted you to be informed of such matters. Your mother might not have been from Boston, but she was a fine girl just the same, from an excellent family, and I regard your care as a sacred trust. I'm sure if they were alive, they would wish you a very happy birthday and tell you how proud they are of you. Stand up straight, Margaret. Nothing is less appealing than stooped shoulders."

"Thank you, Aunt Grace," Meg said, trying to unstoop her shoulders.

"Because it is your birthday, you may stay up until midnight," Aunt Grace said. "The band has been hired to play only until eleven-thirty. I know many of your friends have parties that last until one or two o'clock, but I do not approve of that sort of revelry for a girl so young. You must dance with any of the young men who ask you.

I'm sure they all will, because it's your birthday, and they will be disappointed if you seem to favor one of them over the others. You will be allowed one glass of champagne, when the toast is made. You are to thank each person who brings you a gift, and those who do not, you must thank as well, for attending the party. Tomorrow you will spend writing thank-you notes for whatever gifts you may receive. You are not to wander off from the party with any of your friends. I want to know where you are at all times. If you need to excuse yourself, please inform me first."

"Yes, Aunt Grace," Meg said.

"You're mumbling again," Aunt Grace replied. "I trust you won't spend the evening mumbling and stooping, Margaret. It is your birthday, and people will expect to see you proud and tall. In addition, they'll want to hear you when you say your various pleasantries. Now, put on your dress, and meet me downstairs. I want you ready to greet your guests as they arrive."

"Yes, Aunt Grace," Meg said, and watched with relief as her aunt left the room. At least she hadn't been forced to open the box while Grace was there.

Maybe this time it'll be all right, she thought, but one look at the dress killed that fantasy. It was pink, a color Meg hated, because she blushed so often, and wearing pink seemed to emphasize her embarrassment. Pink chiffon with endless ruffles. Meg was not one for looking at *Vogue*, but even she knew ruffles were all wrong. It was a dress for a little girl. It even had a ruffled collar. The black velvet dress she'd worn when she was eleven was more sophisticated than this.

Meg put on the dress, and glanced at herself as best she could in the mirror over the bureau. Aunt Grace regarded full-length mirrors as an invitation to vanity, and refused to have one in her home. At that moment, Meg was just as glad. As awful as the dress was, it was comforting not to be able to see a complete view. Pink with a ruffled collar and puffed sleeves, and worst of all, even worse than all those ruffles, a bow to tie around her waist. The only thing you could do with a dress like that was burn it.

Meg allowed herself one moment to dream about wearing a different dress to her party, not that the rest of her wardrobe was so much better. But even if it had been, she was stuck with the pink ruffles for the evening. Aunt Grace had allowed her no alternatives.

She brushed her hair so hard she began to cry, then stopped, put on the white shoes that Aunt Grace had also insisted on, and the white gloves to complete the outfit, and went downstairs. No one had arrived yet, thank goodness.

"Very pretty," Aunt Grace said, checking Meg out. "You took such a long time, though, I thought you were putting on makeup."

"It was hard to get to all the buttons," Meg replied.

"You should have rung for Mary," Aunt Grace said.

"I figured she must be busy," Meg said. "Preparing for the party."

"You do not need to worry about what a maid is busy with," Aunt Grace said. "They're paid very well to do what we ask them to. I would have assumed that that, at least, your mother taught you."

Meg could feel herself blushing. "I'm sorry," she said, although she was unsure what she was apologizing for.

"Don't mope," Aunt Grace said. "This is your birthday. What will your guests think if they see you standing there looking so gloomy?"

Meg trusted that was a rhetorical question, since she had no idea how to answer it.

"Go outside now, and wait for the guests," Aunt Grace said. "I'll speak with Delman to make sure everything is in order."

"Thank you, Aunt Grace," Meg said. It seemed to her that was all she ever said, "Thank you" and "I'm sorry." No wonder she mumbled, with such a restricted vocabulary.

She stood in the garden, in front of the bar, and blushed when she felt the bartender's eyes on her. He was a year-rounder, hired for these occasions, and Meg had seen him at parties she'd attended.

"Nice dress," he said. "How old are you? Fourteen?"

"Sixteen," she choked out.

"Oh," he said. "Sorry."

Meg nodded, and walked away from him. The bartender wasn't half as sorry as she was. What a dump, she thought. What a dumpy dumpy dump. The words proved no comfort at all.

Then the guests began arriving, and although Meg was sure their looks were full of pity for her, at least there were a lot of people, and she didn't feel unprotected anymore. Aunt Grace stood by her side, and made sure she said thank you to everybody.

"Hi, Meg," Tinker Thomas said as she came over, carrying a large, promising box.

"Her name is Margaret," Aunt Grace declared, and Meg took a certain pleasure in seeing Tinker blush.

"I meant Margaret," Tinker said. "Hi, Margaret."

"Hello, Margaret," Aunt Grace said. "We do not approve of slang here."

Tinker clenched her teeth, and Meg's pleasure in the moment evaporated. She liked Tinker, and thought Tinker liked her, and now Tinker would avoid her or feel sorry for her or simply not bother to be her friend. "Hello, Margaret," she said. "Happy birthday."

"Thank you, Tinker," Meg said, and watched helplessly as Tinker ran from her side to join some of the other kids. Meg could see them all staring at her, and knew they were laughing at her, at her dress, at her party, at her obvious misery.

"Hello, Margaret."

"Hello, Clark," Meg said, smiling at the one true friend she had among the party guests.

"I brought you this," he said. "Happy birthday."

"Thank you," Meg said. "Thank you for coming."

"I wouldn't have missed it," he said. "Hello, Miss Winslow."

"Clark," Aunt Grace said, and jutted her cheek out for Clark to kiss. He did, with an ease that Meg envied. Clark Bradford was eighteen, and had grown up in Boston. In many ways, he knew Aunt Grace better than she did, and maybe because she wasn't his aunt, he even seemed to like her. It occurred to Meg then that she might marry Clark. It made sense. Aunt Grace would approve, as would Clark's family, and Clark, she was sure, loved her. It would be nice to have a husband who wasn't afraid of Aunt Grace. Maybe Clark would propose to her that very night, pink ruffles and all. If she were engaged, that would make her special. She would feel protected if she were engaged.

She smiled at the thought, and Clark smiled back at her. "I hope you'll save me a dance," he said.

"Of course I will," Meg said. She could talk to Clark. He didn't frighten her. They'd played together when they were children, and her parents had gone up to Boston for holidays and family occasions. Clark was safe and appropriate and he loved her. Meg immediately felt better about things.

"Oh no," Clark said. "My father has his camera out again. I apologize for him, Miss Winslow. Ever since he got the camera for his birthday, he takes it with him wherever he goes."

"Motion pictures?" Aunt Grace said.

"Home movies," Clark said. "Dad, really. Do you have to point that thing at us?"

"Smile, Margaret," Mr. Bradford said, and Meg did as she was told. "Very good," he said. "Lovely party, Grace. Happy birthday, Margaret. Many happy returns and all that. I'll be sure to film you while you're dancing with Clark."

"Thank you," Meg said.

Clark grinned at her, and moved up the line. Meg continued to stand by Grace, accept her presents, and say her thanks, but her mind was on Clark. She didn't know why she'd never thought about marrying him before, but maybe marriage was one of those things you didn't think about until you were sixteen.

"Happy birthday, Margaret."

"Thank you, Isabelle," Meg said. Isabelle Sinclair looked wonderful. She was wearing a pale green strapless gown with not a single ruffle on it.

"Happy birthday, Margaret," Robert Sinclair said. He was Isabelle's older brother, and Margaret knew he would ask her to dance that evening as a courtesy.

"Thank you, Robert," she said.

"I hope you don't mind," Robert said. "I brought along a friend of mine. He's staying with us this summer. Margaret Winslow, I'd like you to meet Nick Sebastian."

CHAPTER THREE

This is the handsomest man I've ever seen, Meg thought, and then just as quickly she thought, but that doesn't matter, and the two thoughts bumped into each other and made her blush. She felt like a fool standing there, turning red in that ridiculous dress, with Aunt Grace standing by her side, making sure she didn't slouch or mumble or forget to thank people. He'll hate me, she thought, and then she couldn't remember his name, or why it was important that he not hate her, and she wished she could vanish, and she wished the moment could last forever.

"Let's dance," he said.

"But I have to stand on line," she replied. Did she mumble? Probably.

"Do you?" he asked.

Meg considered his question. "No," she said. "I don't, do I."

He stared at her and she stared back, and she knew

she wasn't blushing anymore. He took her hand, and led her away from the line, away from Aunt Grace. The band was playing Gershwin. They began to dance.

"I don't know your name," Meg admitted. "I heard it, but I guess I didn't listen hard enough."

"Nick Sebastian," he said. "Do people really call you Margaret?"

"My aunt does," Meg said.

"I'll call you Daisy," Nick said. "You should be called Daisy."

"That's what my parents called me," Meg said. "Most people call me Meg. Aunt Grace insists on Margaret."

"May I call you Daisy, then?" Nick asked.

Meg nodded. She couldn't get over how wonderful it felt to be in his arms. She prayed he wanted to have his way with her.

"Robert and Isabelle said something about a birthday," Nick declared. "Yours, I take it."

Meg nodded.

"I should have brought something," he said.

"You brought me my name," Meg said. "That's a very special gift."

"I want to give you more than that," he said. "But there'll be other birthdays. We'll dance on each of them, I promise."

"Don't tease," Meg said.

"You know I'm not," Nick replied. "What birthday is this, Daisy?"

"Sixteen," she said. Please let that be the right answer, she thought.

Nick shook his head. "You're older than that," he said. "I can see it in your eyes."

Meg thought about the hideous baby dress Aunt Grace

had forced her to wear, and she pledged at that very moment to spend the rest of her life with Nick Sebastian. She intended to tell him that but Clark tapped Nick on the shoulder, and cut in on the dance.

"Do you know him?" Clark asked her. Meg felt herself inch away from Clark, stiffen her body just slightly, turn back into Meg Winslow, stoops and mumbles and all.

"He's a friend of the Sinclairs'," she said. "Robert introduced us."

"He's a bit pushy, don't you think?" Clark said, being sure to lead as they danced. Meg hated it that Clark led. Not that she'd minded Nick leading. "There were people on line waiting to wish you happy birthday."

"They'll know where to find her," Nick said, tapping Clark right back, and stealing Meg away from him before Clark had the chance to react. "Daisy, may I?"

"Who's Daisy?" Clark asked, but they didn't wait to answer. They left him sputtering on the dance floor, as they ran, hand in hand, away from the party guests.

"This is terrible," Meg said, when they'd reached a safe distance. They could hear the sounds of the party, but they knew they couldn't be seen. "Aunt Grace will be so angry."

"I'm sorry," Nick said. "I needed to be alone with you."

"I know," Meg said, and then she laughed. She couldn't remember the last time she'd laughed like that. "I'm not sorry. The hell with Aunt Grace." She waited for the gods of gratitude to strike her down, but the only thing that happened was the band kept playing, and people still danced. The gods have the night off, she thought. I have never been so happy in my life.

"I know you don't know me," Nick said.

"You don't know me either," Meg said.

"I know who you are," he replied. "In some ways I know how you got here. Robert and Isabelle told me a few details. Margaret Winslow of the Beacon Hill Winslows. Your parents died in an accident a few years ago. You go to school with Isabelle. You do well academically; you're fairly popular. You live with your aunt, Grace Winslow. People treat Grace Winslow with respect. They do not steal her niece from under her nose."

"It's such a terrifying nose," Meg said. "I remember even when I was little, Aunt Grace's nose scared me."

"I don't want you to be frightened ever again," Nick said. "I'll do everything I can to protect you."

"What can I do for you?" Meg asked. "I want to do something too."

"You can love me," Nick said.

Meg laughed. "That's too easy," she said. "I do that already."

Then Nick smiled, and Meg realized all those wonderful flirty words were true, that everything they'd both been saying, they meant. She looked then, really hard, at Nick, tried to see who it was she felt so instantly connected to, tried to understand what it was about him that made her feel more eager to live than she'd ever dreamed. But all she could see was he loved her, and for the moment, that was all she needed to see.

"What's your middle name?" she asked. She wanted to know his complete name. He required a full identity, this man she loved.

"George," he said. "I hate it."

"I hate my dress," she replied.

"We can burn it," he said. "We can turn it into ashes."

"We'll do the same with your name," she said. "We'll print it on a piece of paper and tear it into a hundred pieces and put it on the fire, and let it burn. And then you won't be George anymore."

He kissed her then, and Meg was so surprised that she shifted awkwardly, and he thought she was resisting. "I'm sorry, Daisy," he said.

"Oh don't be," she said. "Don't ever be sorry again." She yearned to kiss him, but before she had the chance, Clark came storming over to them.

"What the hell do you think you're doing?" he asked, and Meg was uncertain which one of them he was speaking to, until she saw him grab Nick by his jacket collar as though intending to punch him.

Nick merely shook him off. "I don't think we've been introduced," he said. "I'm Nick Sebastian."

"I don't care if you're Santa Claus," Clark replied. "You have some nerve dragging Meg off like that. Her aunt is furious. And I imagine Isabelle Sinclair isn't any too pleased either."

Nick laughed, but there was no warmth in the sound. "Isabelle doesn't matter. Neither do you nor Aunt Grace. Daisy is all that matters."

"Who's Daisy?" Clark asked again.

Meg found herself standing so tall Aunt Grace would have to look up to her. "I am," she said.

"What's gotten into you?" Clark asked. "Have you been hitting the champagne?"

"I'm happy, Clark," Meg said. "That's your problem. You've never seen me happy before."

"You won't stay happy once Grace gets through with

you," Clark said. "Look you, Sebastian, whatever, if you really care for Meg the way you claim you do, you'd better bring her back to the party and apologize like crazy to her aunt. Otherwise Grace will take it out on Meg for what you've done."

"Let her," Meg said. "I don't care."

"You heard her, Clark," Nick said. "Will you leave us alone now, please?"

"I don't know who you are," Clark said. "And I don't know what you're doing to Meg to make her act this way, but I'm going to tell Grace, and that will be the end of that. Meg, I'll do what I can for you, but Grace is furious already, and your best chance is to go back to her alone and apologize like the blue devil."

Meg shook her head. "Aunt Grace can't do anything to me anymore," she said. "Nick will protect me."

"It's drugs," Clark said. "You slipped her some kind of drug, didn't you. If you hurt one hair of her head, I'll kill you." He paused, and Meg used all her self-control to keep from laughing at him.

"Calm down," Nick said. "You've done your good deed for the evening. You've earned your merit badge. Go back to the party and have a good time. It's been a pleasure knowing you. Good night, Clark."

"Meg, please," Clark said, but Meg took Nick's hand in hers, and entwined her fingers with his. Clark looked at them, shook his head with funereal solemnity, and walked back to the party.

"We don't have much time," Nick said. "May I see you tomorrow?"

"Of course," she said. "We'll find a way."

Nick nodded. "I love you," he said. "Do you know that?"

Meg smiled her reply.

"We'll get married, you know," Nick said. "I suppose we'll have to wait a couple of years, but we will get married. I'll make you so happy, Daisy. I'll give you everything you want."

"You already have," Meg said. She looked up at him, to commit his face to her memory, and saw a small scar by his right ear.

Nick turned his head slightly away from her. "I'm imperfect," he said. "Damaged goods."

"How did it happen?" Meg asked.

"The truth?" Nick asked, and Meg realized he wasn't being flippant.

"The truth," she said. "You can tell me anything."

"My stepfather hit me there," he said. "With a skillet. We were fighting and he wanted to kill me. My mother was so scared she called the police, and I wound up living in foster care for a few months. No one knows that about me, none of that. No one. They think my parents . . . they think I'm respectable." Nick looked straight into Meg's eyes. "You have power over me now," he said. "I've trusted you with who I really am."

"I won't fail you," she said, and she kissed him. "No matter what, I won't ever fail you."

"Daisy," Nick said, and there was so much in just that one word, so much past and future, that Meg felt free of all fears and burdens, yet tied to time, to place, and reality.

"It will be all right," she said. "I never knew that before, but now I do."

"We'll save each other," Nick said. "That's it, isn't it."

"Of course it is," Meg said. There was so much she

wanted to tell him, even more she wanted to hear, but the sound of footsteps interrupted them.

"You'd better get out of here," Clark said to Nick. "Grace has called the police. If you don't want to get arrested, you'd better leave right now."

"Arrested?" Nick said, and he laughed again. Meg marveled that his laugh could be so cold when his smile was radiant.

"The police," Clark said. "Meg, please. There's going to be awful scandal."

Meg laughed. "I imagine there will be," she said.

"He's nobody," Clark said. "Robert says he hardly knows him. He isn't even a year-rounder."

"I love him, Clark," Meg said, and it seemed odd that Clark should be the first person she told, but then it was right. Clark was her friend. In his own foolish, feeble way, he cared about her.

"You don't even know him," Clark said. "Meg, come back with me, and you, you get out of here if you know what's good for you."

"I do know what's good for me," Nick replied, and he held Meg's hand.

"The police, Meg," Clark said. "Do you really want this guy arrested?"

"No," Meg said. "Nick, you'd better go."

"I don't care," he said. "I don't want to leave you."

"I'll be fine," she said.

"No," he said. "I'll take you back to the party. That's the least I can do."

Meg thought about the scene Grace was likely to make and shuddered.

"You don't have to be scared of her," Nick said. "Come on, Daisy. Let me take you back."

"I'll go with you," Clark said. "Meg, you don't have to protect him. You can tell Grace the truth, that he made you leave with him."

"I know what the truth is, Clark," Meg said. She walked hand in hand with Nick back to the party. The band stopped playing as they approached.

"I guess they don't know the death march," Nick whispered. Meg laughed out loud. Clark looked grimly determined to guard Meg from further contamination.

"I bring you back your niece, Miss Winslow," Nick proclaimed as they rejoined the party. "Safe and sound."

"Get off of my property this minute!" Aunt Grace shouted. "I've called the police to chase you away!"

"I'm leaving," Nick said, but he seemed in no hurry to go.

"Margaret, go to your room immediately," Grace said. "Your behavior has been shameful. We will discuss your punishment later."

"No," Nick said. "You won't punish her."

"Will you shut up," Clark whispered. "You're only making things worse."

"It was my fault," Nick said. "I made her go with me. She didn't want to. She begged me not to, but there were things I had to say to her, and I needed privacy. Daisy, Margaret, was a victim. You don't punish a victim."

"Nick," Meg said.

"I'll stay if you want me arrested," Nick said. "If that will give you pleasure, fine. But you have to promise not to do anything to Margaret. It's her birthday. This party is for her. Isn't the embarrassment she feels punishment enough?"

"I don't know who you are, young man," Grace said. "But I intend to find out."

"Do you promise not to hurt Margaret?" Nick asked.

"I'll promise you nothing," Grace said.

"There, there, Grace," Clark's father said. "This has all been very unpleasant. Let the boy go, and let's forget the entire incident. Margaret's unharmed, no damage has been done. We don't really want to see this incident in the papers, do we?"

Grace stood still for a moment, considering the situation.

"I'm sorry, Aunt Grace," Meg said, but the words weren't hateful, the way they usually were. She could say anything if it protected Nick. "I'll apologize to all the guests if you want."

"Daisy," Nick said, but Meg shook her head slightly, to force him into silence.

"Go," Grace said to Nick. "And don't ever return here again."

Nick held Meg's hand for one last moment. "Tomorrow," he whispered so quietly she could barely hear him.

She nodded back as imperceptibly. Nick smiled at her again, and then turned to Aunt Grace. "Thank you for having me," he said. "It's been a lovely evening. Good night, everybody."

"Wait up, Sebastian," Robert Sinclair said. "I'll go with you."

"Fine," Nick said. The two young men walked out of the party together. Meg waited to burst into tears at the sight of his departure, but found she was too happy to cry.

"What exactly happened?" Grace demanded, as Meg humbly but with good posture faced her.

"We needed to talk," Meg said. "That's all. Clark blew it all out of proportion."

"I did not," Clark said. "Margaret was behaving very peculiarly. I felt it my duty to report it."

"Very noble of you, my son," Clark's father said. "I'll call the police now, Grace, tell them not to bother." He walked back to the house, carrying his camera with him. Meg wondered how much of this amazing evening he had preserved on film.

"I suspect you have been a very bad girl," Aunt Grace said, and Meg realized her aunt had no vocabulary for what she felt. It gave Meg a sense of power, which she tried not to show.

"I suspect I have been," Meg replied.

"When you write your notes tomorrow, you will include an apology to every single guest," Aunt Grace said. "You should probably apologize to each of them in person, but this party has been memorable enough without that for people to gossip about."

"Gossip," Meg said. It had never occurred to her that she was capable of doing anything interesting enough for people to gossip about.

"I blame this all on your mother," Aunt Grace said. "She was a nice enough girl, but from New York, and New Yorkers have no real sense of appropriate behavior."

"They certainly don't," Clark said. "I bet that guy . . ."

"Don't say 'guy,' " Grace said.

"That man then, whatever he says his name is, I bet he's from New York," Clark said. "Or someplace even worse."

Nick hadn't said where he was from, Meg thought. Not that it mattered. He knew where she was, so he could find her and be with her, and rescue her forever. Knowing all that made her feel strong and reckless.

"Come on, Clark," she said. "If you're so determined to dance with me, let's dance."

"That's not a very nice invitation," Clark said, but he followed Meg onto the dance floor. She laughed silently from the pleasure of leading.

CHAPTER FOUR

The doorbell rang at ten after nine the next morning. Delman, the butler, answered it. Nick Sebastian, holding a large bouquet of flowers, smiled at him.

"I've come to see Miss Winslow," he declared.

"Miss Winslow?" Delman asked, in a voice that had shriveled many a lesser man.

"Miss Grace Winslow," Nick said, standing his ground.

Meg, who had observed all this from the relative safety of the morning room, swiftly entered the hallway. "I thought I had dreamed you," she whispered as Delman left to speak to Aunt Grace.

Nick nodded. "I know," he replied. "You're everything I've ever dreamed."

Meg yearned to embrace him, but knew she couldn't, not while they were waiting for Aunt Grace. She held herself in, trying not to smile, not to faint from pleasure or exhaustion. She'd gotten no sleep the night before, her mind too filled with images of Nick, and constant warning voices urging her to forget the whole thing. Margaret Louise Winslow wasn't the sort of person to fall in love at first sight. It must not have happened, at least not the way she dreamed it had. But there Nick was, and he still loved her. Meg wished there was someone she could thank, but the only person she could think of was her mother.

"Let me do the talking," Nick whispered to her. "And don't mind a thing I say. It's for both of us."

Meg nodded. She knew she could trust Nick, she knew she already had, letting him arouse feelings in her she'd buried for years.

Nick gave her an almost frantic look. "I'll call you Margaret," he whispered. "But I know you're Daisy."

"All right," Meg whispered back. There was no time for further conspiracy, as they could both hear Aunt Grace's autocratic footsteps.

"Yes, Mr. Sebastian?" she said.

"May I come in?" Nick asked. "I'd like to give you these flowers."

"Very well," Aunt Grace said. "Come in, make your apologies, and then leave."

"Thank you," Nick said. He handed her the bouquet. "I would have been here earlier, but I had to wait for the florist to open. I do want to apologize, Miss Winslow, for any embarrassment I might have caused you or your party guests last night. I behaved thoughtlessly, and in the cold light of morning, I am deeply ashamed."

Meg checked him out. Nick did look ashamed. She wondered if she would ever see that look again, and somehow doubted it. Shame seemed as unnatural to him as his harsh laughter.

"A pretty speech," Aunt Grace said.

"It ought to be," Nick said. "I worked on it all night."

"You are a very clever man," Aunt Grace said. "I have accepted your flowers and shall think about your apology. You may leave."

"I'd rather stay," Nick said, and Meg noticed how he had inched himself deeper into the house. "Is there someplace we might talk?"

"There are many places," Aunt Grace said. "That doesn't mean that you are invited into any of them."

Nick smiled, but it wasn't the smile Meg had fallen in love with the night before. This smile was related to his laughter. "You are a very clever woman," he said. "Can we concede that point, and go on from there?"

"And why should we?" Aunt Grace asked.

"Because we both care for Margaret," Nick replied. "We have that common interest."

"You hardly know the girl," Aunt Grace said. "You only met her last night. How can you possibly claim to have feelings for her?"

"You only met me last night," Nick pointed out. "And already you dislike me."

Was it possible? Had Aunt Grace actually blushed? If Nick did nothing else for Meg, he'd given her the gift of that moment.

"Come into the morning room," Aunt Grace said. "If this must be discussed, let us discuss it immediately and then be done with it."

"Thank you," Nick said. Aunt Grace led the way, so he was free to flash Meg a V for Victory sign. Meg covered her mouth to keep from laughing.

Since Aunt Grace hadn't told her to stay away, Meg went with them to the morning room. She knew she was being unwise, but she couldn't bear the thought of being parted from Nick. It would have been especially hard knowing he was in the house with her. She wanted to sit down next to him, but that would truly have been folly, so she stood inconspicuously by the door, where Aunt Grace wouldn't be able to make eye contact with her. Nick sat facing both Meg and Aunt Grace, but the focus of his attention was on the enemy.

"Now, what do you have to say?" Aunt Grace asked. "Make it brief. I am a busy woman."

"I've apologized already for my misconduct last night," Nick began. "It was an impulsive act, and that's unusual for me. I am not an impulsive person."

"It was perhaps a drunken act?" Aunt Grace said.

Was Nick angry? Meg suspected that he was, by the additional level of calm in his voice when he replied. "No," he said. "I was not drunk. I almost never drink, and last night was no exception."

"Then how can you explain your bizarre behavior?" Aunt Grace asked. Did that mean she believed him? Meg could have testified to Nick's sobriety, except she'd felt drunk herself with joy and anticipation.

"The party was noisy," Nick said. "Through no fault of yours. Parties tend to be noisy. I was dancing with your niece, and we were cut in on. I knew that would happen all night long. Margaret is a pretty girl, and last night was her birthday. I wanted a chance to speak with her quietly, and the only way I could see doing that was removing her from the party. So we left."

"And what did you need to say to her that was so pressing?" Aunt Grace asked.

Meg thought back to their conversation the night before. Be careful, she willed Nick.

"I needed to say that I loved her," Nick replied. "What I did say was that I hoped to see her again."

"Love?" Aunt Grace said. The word sounded like poison coming from her mouth.

Nick looked straight at Grace. "I've never loved any other girl before," he said. "So it's possible I'm putting the wrong label on my feelings. But the level of my emotions was intense, and frankly, it hasn't abated since. I won't lie to you about that."

"So you claim you love her," Aunt Grace declared. "As though that allows any form of antisocial behavior."

"Of course not," Nick said. "I'm here, aren't I? I've brought you flowers and apologies and honesty. I will tell you anything you want to know about me, reassure you in any way I can. The last thing I want is for you to be worried about Margaret. I know what a burden it must be to raise an orphaned niece."

"It isn't always easy," Grace conceded.

"My parents are dead also," Nick said. "And I would give anything to have an aunt or an uncle like you, one willing to provide not just a home, but love and caring. Margaret is very fortunate."

"That she is," Aunt Grace said. "Although she doesn't always behave as though she knows it."

"Perhaps not to you," Nick replied. "But when we spoke about you last night, it was obvious how deep her affection and gratitude run."

"Am I to believe then that after you professed your undying love, the two of you sat around and discussed me?" Aunt Grace asked.

Nick laughed. "You came up in conversation," he said. "I admit you weren't our primary focus."

And then the strangest thing happened. Aunt Grace

laughed also. Meg pressed hard against the wall to keep herself from falling.

"You have a certain charm," Aunt Grace declared. "A dangerous attribute, but an appealing one. What else do you have to offer my niece?"

"I respect her, if that's what you mean," Nick said. "Her purity isn't at risk."

"That's a pretty speech," Aunt Grace said. "But I meant more mundane things. Family. Social position. Who exactly are you? I'd never seen you before last night. Your family cannot possibly come from Boston."

"We don't," Nick said. "My parents, as I mentioned before, are dead. I'm a sophomore at Princeton, or I will be in September. I met Robert Sinclair there, and his parents were kind enough to invite me to their home for the summer."

"You have no family of your own?" Aunt Grace asked.

"My father died during the war," Nick said. "On D-day. My mother's family came from the South, but she'd moved to the Midwest to live with my father, and after his death, she chose to stay there. She remarried after the war, but my stepfather and I never got along, and following my mother's death, I moved out of his home. Mr. Wilson, a teacher at my high school, took me in. He was a very kind man, and I owe him a great deal. I stayed with him until I graduated high school. It worked out well for both of us, actually. He developed cancer, and I was able to help him during his final months. I don't know if you know anything about cancer, Miss Winslow, and what it does to you, but it's a disease best faced not alone. Mr. Wilson had no family, so he left me his estate. I sold the house, and I'm using that money to pay for my college education. It's not a glamorous story, but it's the truth, and it's what got me here. The Sinclairs find me perfectly respectable. My grades at Princeton are A's, except for one B I got in philosophy. Frankly, I should have gotten an A in that as well, but I didn't put enough effort into my term paper. I love your niece. I must, or else I never would have bothered to come here today. Do I have your permission to see her again?"

"You are a good-looking boy," Grace said. "And I liked your little speech, especially the part about your philosophy grade. But you still haven't told me a thing about your family, except that they're all dead. You have no grandparents, no aunts or uncles? You come from nowhere?"

"I come from Iowa," Nick said. "My mother's family came from South Carolina. My mother was an only child. Her father was a banker, but he died when I was five, and my grandmother died shortly thereafter. My mother had cousins there, but except for my mother's funeral, I haven't had any contact with them. My father had a brother, but he died in the war as well. He was a young man, unmarried. My father's mother was devastated by the loss of her only two sons, and she died near the end of the war. My father's father had owned a small factory, but with no sons to run it, the factory was sold. Since he didn't approve of my mother's remarriage, he left both of us out of his will, and his estate, when he passed away, went to some cousins of his. They felt a certain amount of guilt about the hand that had been dealt me. Not enough to do anything about it, mind you. Just enough so they chose to cut off all connections with me. I am not besieged by family. My roots are respectable, but I'm alone in this world. Or at least I was until yesterday."

"I shall have to check all this out," Aunt Grace said. "I can hardly trust a stranger with my niece, especially one who admits to being without family or money."

"I have money enough to get through school," Nick said. "Money enough to buy you flowers. And I had family. You can hardly hold it against me if my parents died. You don't hold it against Margaret."

"Margaret has family," Aunt Grace said. "But it is true, she has no money. If you've come digging for gold, I suggest you locate a more prosperous young lady."

"She's only sixteen," Nick said. "If I were digging for gold, I'd find someone a bit older. I'm not a fool, Miss Winslow."

"No," Aunt Grace said. "I can see that."

"Then may I have your permission to take Margaret for a walk this morning?" he asked. "We'll stay on your grounds, if you would feel more comfortable that way."

"I would indeed," Aunt Grace replied. "Very well. Have your walk. Perhaps once the two of you look at each other without moonlight this foolish infatuation will end."

"Thank you," Nick said. He rose from his chair, paused for a moment, then nodded farewell to Grace. Meg slipped out of the room behind him. They walked out of the house quietly, and with dignity, and it wasn't until they had reached a safe distance on the beach that they whooped and hollered and hugged each other with abandon.

"Kiss me," Nick said, and Meg did, not caring if Aunt Grace and her legion of servants were all watching with binoculars from the back windows. "I didn't think I could survive that," he said. "All that time with you in the room, and not being able to touch you, to hold you."

"I wanted to sit by your side," Meg said. "But I knew how angry that would make her."

"She was angry enough," Nick said. "And she'll be angry again soon." He stood for a moment, then he pressed Meg to him, and they kissed again. But then he backed off.

Meg looked at him. "What's the matter?" she asked. She knew she had no experience kissing, and undoubtedly Nick could write a book on the subject, he was so good-looking, but everything had felt right to her.

Nick smiled, and it was his smile again. "Nothing's the matter," he replied. "Well, everything is, but except for that, nothing. It's just I want you so much, and the one honest thing I said to your aunt was that I respected your purity."

"The hell with my purity," Meg said, dazzled by her own daring.

"No," Nick said. "Besides, there's a lot I have to say to you, and we don't have much time. Walk with me, the way I told your aunt we would."

"Kiss me first," Meg demanded, and she was pleased with how quickly Nick acceded.

"I love you, Daisy," Nick said. "I thought you were beautiful last night in that ridiculous dress, but now that I see you in daylight . . ." He paused long enough to kiss her one more time. "Do you still love me?"

"Do you doubt it?" Meg asked.

Nick shook his head. "I just can't get over it," he said. "How perfect you are."

"Me?" Meg said. "I'm not perfect. I mumble and I stoop and I'm not nearly as grateful as I should be. And I really don't have any money. Just a little trust fund."

"That's more than I have," Nick said. "It's more than

we'll need. Maybe I wouldn't have fallen in love if you did have money. Did you ever think of that?"

"I haven't had a chance to think of anything," Meg replied. "Except how much I wanted you to be real."

"I'm real," Nick said. "But Daisy, listen to me. I just told your aunt a packful of lies. And she's bound to find out, starting with a phone call to Mrs. Sinclair. I am persona non grata there right now. As a matter of fact, I was kicked out first thing this morning. Before breakfast. If your aunt's called already, and she probably has, she must know that."

"Where are you staying?" Meg asked.

"I found a room at an inn for a day or two," Nick said. "When I get a chance, I'll find a boardinghouse to stay in for the rest of the summer. I'm not leaving you, Daisy. I have enough money, if I'm careful with it, to make it through until graduation. Free room and board was a blessing, but it wasn't a requirement. I just have to be careful, that's all."

"I wish I could give you some money," Meg said. "It's my fault, after all, that the Sinclairs kicked you out. I can give you the check Uncle Marcus sent me for my birthday. Would that help?"

"Oh Daisy," Nick said, and he kissed her again. Meg wasn't sure whether that meant yes or no, but she knew she didn't care. "Forget your money," he said. "Whatever you do, you must never give me any of your money. We're doomed if you do."

Meg nodded. "But if you won't take my money or my purity, what do I have to give you?" she asked.

"Your love," he said. "Your trust. Although you may withdraw that as well."

"I trust you," Meg said, and she was surprised by the

voice she said it with. It wasn't her usual scared-little-girl voice. There was a woman's trust behind those words, a woman's strength as well.

"How much truth can you take?" Nick asked her. "Don't lie to me, Daisy. There's a lot, and it's ugly, and I'll tell you only as much as you want to know."

"I want to know everything," Meg replied, and again, it wasn't a schoolgirl speaking. "I love you, Nicky, and you're a part of me. There's nothing you can tell me I can't understand."

Nick shook his head. "I want to believe you," he said.

"If I can trust you, you can trust me," Meg declared. She squeezed his hand with hers and hoped that some of her faith in him came through.

"You have to forget everything I said to your aunt," Nick declared. "All those pretty lies."

"You didn't lie about your feelings," Meg said. "What else matters?"

"A lot else," Nick replied. "Especially to your aunt. Let's see. Out of all that romantic gobbledygook, the only truth was that my mother's dead. Oh, and that my stepfather and I don't get along. But you already knew that."

"There must have been some truth," Meg said. "You couldn't have made it all up."

"I did, pretty much," Nick said. "It's the story I tell everybody at Princeton. No one there ever bothered to check it out, but your aunt will, and she'll find out a lot of ugly things about me, and she'll make a big point of telling you. I want you to hear it from me first. Maybe it'll hurt you less that way."

"I love you, Nicholas George Sebastian," Meg said. "Now tell me all your ugly truths."

Nick laughed, and it was that harsh, humorless laugh that Meg dreaded. "For starters, that wasn't the name I was born with," he declared. "I had it changed legally before I started Princeton."

"What was your name then?" Meg asked. She marveled that none of this concerned her. The only thing she wanted was to alleviate Nick's pain.

"George Nicholas Keefer," Nick said. "Nobody ever called me George, though. I was always Nick."

"Why did you change it?" Meg asked. "Not that you look like a George Keefer."

"Tell me you love me," Nick said. "I need to hear it again."

"I love you, Nicky," Meg said. "No matter what your name is. No matter who you really are. I love you."

"I changed my name because I hated George Keefer," Nick said. "I hated who he was, what he'd been through. I figured a new name, a new life, new chances. I was right about that too. Nick Sebastian gets treated differently than George Keefer."

"Is that all?" Meg asked. "Is that your full confession?"

Nick looked out toward the ocean. It was a foggy, gray morning and visibility was poor. Meg wondered what he was staring at, why he could no longer face her.

"Family means everything to your aunt," he said.

"My aunt's a fool," Meg replied. She wanted to laugh with the knowledge.

"I wish she were," Nick declared. "Things would be so much easier if she were. But family is important. Take it from someone who doesn't have any."

"I don't have any either," Meg said.

Nick shook his head. "You don't understand," he replied. "It's my fault. I'm doing this badly. It's just I'm going to tell you things I've never told anybody before, and it frightens me. But you have to be honest. If what I say disgusts you, if it makes you love me the less, or not at all, then be honest about it. I can live with pain. I have experience."

Meg wanted to reassure him, but she knew that wasn't what he needed. "Tell me," she said instead. "I can't know how I'll feel until you do."

Nick continued to look away from her. "I'm illegitimate," he said. "My birth certificate says 'father unknown.' "

Meg tried to understand what that meant, not just to the world, but to Nick. She wanted to ask if it was true, was his father unknown, but she didn't dare.

"I think that's the worst of it," Nick said. "To me it is, anyway. Are you still there, Daisy?"

"Oh yes," Meg replied. "I'm still here."

"It's a lie, the part about him being unknown," Nick said. "Not my lie, though. My mother knew who my father was. He was her boss. She was a secretary, and it was her first job, she was younger than I am, and I don't know, he seduced her. Maybe he raped her. I wouldn't put it past him. Anyway, however the courtship took place, she ended up pregnant, and naturally he didn't want to have anything to do with her after that. Your aunt talks so much about family, about social position. My father had plenty of both, and he wasn't about to see them jeopardized by the arrival of a little bastard. So he paid my mother off. But part of the bargain was she had to put 'father unknown' on the birth certificate. He wasn't taking any chances."

"Oh Nicky," Meg said. She reached out for him, but he refused her offer of comfort.

"My mother had me, and she kept me for as long as

the money held out," Nick continued. "Then she put me in a home for a while, and then she took me out, and relatives took care of me. I bounced around a lot when I was little. None of it was fun. I loved my mother, though, just because she was my mother. Whenever I'd see her, I thought that meant she was taking me to live with her. I really wanted a home. I know you understand that."

Meg nodded.

"Then my mother got married and things got really bad," Nick said, and he laughed that awful laugh of his. "He was a cruel son of a bitch, cruel to me and to my mother. He drank and he liked to hit us. He must have liked to, he did it often enough. But my mother stayed with him, and they had a couple of kids, and that didn't make things any better. Not for me, at any rate. I think he hit my mother a little less once he had a son of his own, but I may be being too charitable. I'm sorry, Daisy. I wish I could be someone perfect. I wish I were appropriate."

"It doesn't matter," Meg said. "No, that isn't true. You are perfect. You are appropriate. If you had a perfect, appropriate past, you might not love me."

"I'd always love you," Nick said. "I always will."

"Good," Meg said. "Because I'll always love you as well. You don't have to tell me the rest if you don't want to."

"I don't want to," Nick said. "But I do have to. There isn't that much anyway. My mother got cancer and died. I was almost sixteen. I doubt those cousins I told your aunt about came to the funeral, but I can't be sure since I didn't go. I wanted to, but my stepfather had a warrant out for my arrest, and I didn't dare show up. He claimed I'd stolen some money, which I hadn't. I meant to, but my mother died before I expected her to, and I never had the chance. That was a very rough time, when she died."

"Did Mr. Wilson take you in right away?" Meg asked. Mr. Wilson was a comforting concept.

"There wasn't any Mr. Wilson," Nick said. "He was a lie too. I wish there'd been. I wish for him, and I wish for a father who died on D-day. But they're both fantasies. I had a year and a half left to go in high school, and I survived. I lived in flophouses and worked any kind of menial job I could get until I graduated."

"But how did you get the money for Princeton?" Meg asked. "How do you have enough money to spend the summer here?"

Nick's smile was filled with pain. "I thought I'd told you the worst," he declared. "And now I find I haven't."

"Tell me," Meg said. "I've gone this far with you. I can manage the rest."

"I went to my father," Nick replied. "And I demanded the money. I figured it was the least he owed me. He figured otherwise. Oh Daisy . . ."

Whatever other confessions Nick was about to make were interrupted by the sight of Clark racing toward them. Meg sighed, but stood her ground against this latest obstacle.

CHAPTER FIVE

"What is it now?" Meg asked as Clark ran over to them. She tried to keep the fury she felt from showing, not yet knowing what sort of effect it would have on Nick.

"Keep away from him, Meg," Clark said. "He's a fraud and a liar and he's probably dangerous."

At first Nick ignored Clark's presence, his mind, Meg assumed, on what he'd been telling her and his fears of her response. But at the word "dangerous," he turned to face Clark.

"You don't belong here," Nick said. "Go home."

"Are you going to let him talk to me that way?" Clark demanded. "Meg, he's the outsider. He's the one who doesn't belong. I'm telling you, he's dangerous. I can feel it. What are you doing with him, anyway?"

Meg thought of a hundred answers to that question, but she wasn't sure she was ready to voice any of them. "We were talking," she said. "That's all."

"Oh," Nick said. "So that's what we were doing."

"What does he mean by that?" Clark asked. "What were you talking about?"

"It's none of your business," Meg said. "Clark, go on home. I don't need you, honestly I don't."

"You don't know what you need," Clark replied. "No, Meg, that's the truth. You've never known. Ever since your parents died, you haven't really known anything about yourself. And now you're so confused, I don't know if even I can save you."

"She doesn't need you to save her," Nick said.

Clark looked as though he wanted to hit Nick, but instead he turned to Meg. "I told you he was a fraud," he said. "Well, he is. I bet he said he was staying with the Sinclairs. He isn't, not anymore. I called up Robert Sinclair this morning, and he says his parents kicked this guy out because of the scene he caused last night."

Nick laughed. "They kicked me out because I wasn't going to serve their function anymore," he declared. "They invited me for the summer to distract Isabelle, keep her from the grocery bagger. And I went along with it. Free room and board at an Eastgate cottage in exchange for a little flirting, the occasional date. It was a fair deal. But once I saw Daisy, I knew I couldn't live up to my end of the bargain, and the Sinclairs knew it too. That hardly makes me Public Enemy Number One."

"There's more to it than that," Clark said. "There has to be."

"Would you really have gone out with Isabelle?" Meg asked.

Nick nodded. "Before," he said. "Before, I would have done almost anything."

"You see what I mean," Clark said. "That's dangerous talk, Meg. Will you forget about this guy, and go back to your aunt's house? You can have a great summer. We'll go sailing and swimming and ride horses and play tennis. There are dances every weekend at the club, and parties, and I'll see to it you aren't bored. You'll forget about this jerk in a minute if you give yourself the chance."

Meg smiled. "But I am giving myself the chance," she declared. "Can't you see, that's just what I'm doing."

"But what do you know about him?" Clark asked.

"I know everything," Meg replied, and whether that was true or not, it felt true, or at least true enough to say to Clark. "Everything that counts."

"And you know what he knows about you?" Clark continued. "He knows you're in line to inherit all of Grace Winslow's money. That's what he knows. He knows you're an heiress, Meg, and that's all he cares about."

"What makes you think Aunt Grace is going to leave me anything?" Meg asked. "Or that I'll even outlive her."

"Don't talk that way," Clark said. "It's bad luck."

Meg laughed.

Clark stared at her. "You haven't told him, have you," he said. "You know everything about him, but I bet he doesn't know a blessed thing about you, except for what your prospects are."

"Told me what?" Nick asked, and for the first time since Clark had arrived, he actually seemed interested in the conversation.

"It's nothing," Meg said. "And it's certainly nothing Clark should know anything about."

"Of course I know," Clark replied. "Marcus Winslow told half the world when it happened. Everybody knows, Meg. Everybody except Mr. Wonderful, that is."

"What does everybody know?" Nick asked. "Daisy,

tell me. I don't ever want to learn anything about you from somebody else."

"It's no big deal," Meg said, and she could no longer remember whether it had been a big deal or not. "After my parents died, I lived with my uncle Marcus for a while, because he had a wife and lots of children, so they thought I'd be better off there, and I hated it. I really hated it, Nicky."

"Did they hurt you?" Nick asked.

"Oh no," Meg said. "Not the way you're thinking. Nothing like that. They tried very hard with me, I know I should be grateful, but I was used to such a different way of life. My parents were wonderful, Nicky. I wish you could have known them."

"They would have put a stop to this right away," Clark said. "Any decent-minded parent would."

"Will you shut up already," Nick said. "What did this uncle do to you, Daisy?"

"What are you suggesting?" Clark asked. "Some sort of gutter behavior your kind is familiar with?"

Meg sighed. "I was very unhappy," she said. "I missed my parents. I still do, but then it was worse, and Uncle Marcus had so many children, and they were all so noisy. My parents were quiet people. I'm a quiet person. They tried very hard with me, but they wanted to turn me into a noisy person so I'd fit in, and I couldn't. I just got quieter, and somehow that made them even noisier. Do you understand?"

"I understand people trying to drag you down to their level," Nick replied. "I understand how hard it is to resist that."

Meg wasn't sure that was just it, but with Clark there, she didn't want to compare and contrast. "No matter what they did for me, I grew unhappier," she said. "That's all. It was as hard for them as it was for me. Uncle Marcus isn't used to failure. And I was his niece, his flesh and blood. He loved my father and he wanted me to be loud and happy, and I was quiet and sad."

"If you don't tell him, I will," Clark said.

"One night I tried to kill myself," Meg said. "All I wanted was to be dead. At least when you're dead, you can be quiet and nobody minds. Uncle Marcus has a house in Newport, that's where they summer, and I got up very late at night, and put on my bathing suit and went swimming. It's a big ocean. I figured there was plenty of water to swallow me up."

"Did you change your mind?" Nick asked.

"I got rescued," Meg said. "There was a couple on the beach and they saw me and swam out and rescued me. I was too tired to fight, too helpless. Afterward, they kept me in bed for a few days, and all kinds of doctors checked me over, and then Uncle Marcus decided I was his first defeat, and I went to live with Aunt Grace."

"You fool," Nick said. "Didn't you know I'd come?"

"Did you know about me?" Meg asked.

Nick took Meg by the hand and embraced her. Meg felt the warmth of his body against hers, and the past five years held no more pain.

"Very pretty," Clark said. "But you can see now she's damaged goods. Why don't you try your luck again with Isabelle Sinclair. Bag boys can't have half your charm."

"They have twice yours," Nick said. "Daisy, there's so much we need to talk about. There's so much I want to do for you."

"You've done it already," Meg replied. "You've loved me."

"Wait a second," Clark said. "Lots of people love you, Meg. They may not call you Daisy but they love you. And they know you, too, and have the same values you have. The only thing he values is a dollar bill."

Nick turned to face Clark. "Who are you, anyway?" he asked. "You keep showing up, like a recurring nightmare."

"I am a nightmare," Clark said. "I'm your conscience, Sebastian, if that's what your name really is. I'm also Meg's protector, and don't you forget it."

"It's Clark something, isn't it," Nick said.

Meg laughed. "His name is Clark Bradford," she said. "And he's a friend of mine." She paused for a moment. "He really is," she said.

Nick looked Clark over. "I didn't realize he was someone you cared about," he said. "I'm sorry, Clark, if I've offended you in any way." He stuck his hand out for Clark to shake.

Clark stared at Nick and moved away from him. "You've offended me in every conceivable way," he declared. "I'd sooner die than shake your hand."

"Fair enough," Nick said, putting his hand down. "But if you change your mind, let me know. I want to like the people Daisy likes. I never want there to be any conflict between us."

"I'll like your friends too," Meg said.

"I don't have friends," Nick said.

"That I can believe," Clark said. "That's probably the first honest thing he's ever told you."

"Go," Meg said to Clark. "I don't know what you think you're accomplishing here, but all you're doing is making me angry. Go home and play with your train set."

"I haven't played with my train set in three years!" Clark said. "And I'm not leaving you alone with Mr. Friendless over here. You may think you're safe, but I know you're not, and I won't leave the two of you alone."

"You're not my chaperon, Clark," Meg said.

"I'm your guardian angel," Clark replied. "You might as well go, Sebastian. I'm sticking with Meg like glue."

"He loves you," Nick said. "I'm glad. He can watch out for you if something happens to me."

"Something's going to happen if you don't get out of here," Clark said.

Meg held Nick's hand. "There's so much more," she said.

"We have time," Nick replied. "Let me walk you back to your aunt's house."

"I'll take her back," Clark said. "Why don't you leave now, and go fortune hunting someplace else. Long Island is good this time of year. Lots of fair game there."

"Are you coming with us?" Nick asked, putting his arm around Meg. She was still surprised at how comfortable she felt there, how right. She wondered if she'd ever get used to it, and almost hoped she wouldn't.

"Step by step," Clark said, and he walked by Meg's side the entire distance. Meg pretended not to notice him, and she honestly felt that Nick didn't. Clark was just there, like the clouds and the waves. When he chattered, he was just a blue jay.

"Miss Winslow would like to see you," Delman announced as they opened the front door. "Mr. Sebastian, that is."

"I'm going with you," Meg declared, and Clark followed them into the morning room.

"I see you brought my niece back safely," Aunt Grace said.

"I saw to that," Clark said. "I kept an eye on him the entire time."

"Thank you, Clark," Grace said. "Mr. Sebastian, in your absence, I called Caroline Sinclair and spoke to her about you."

"And she told you I was no longer staying with them," Nick said.

"She told me that, and more," Grace replied. "She said that while it was true you had met Robert at Princeton, the two of you were not good friends, and Robert had never met any of your family during the year of your acquaintanceship."

"I never claimed he had," Nick said. "I like Robert, he likes me, he knew I was at loose ends for the summer, so he invited me to stay with his family. His parents knew about the invitation. It was originally Mrs. Sinclair's idea. We'd met when the Sinclairs came to visit Robert at school. It didn't seem to bother her then that Robert had never met any of my family. Given that I don't have any family, it would have been hard for him to meet them."

"Are you through?" Aunt Grace asked.

"The question is, are you?" Nick replied.

"Do you want me to throw him out for you?" Clark asked.

Aunt Grace gave Clark the kind of look that shriveled Meg for weeks. Clark didn't seem to hold up to it much better.

"All I know about you is what you told me this morning," Aunt Grace declared. "You started off with lies, and undoubtedly, you continued and finished with lies as well."

"I didn't lie about the Sinclairs," Nick said. "I said that they had invited me to spend the summer there, which was true. I never said I was still staying with them. That would have been untrue."

"You led me to believe you were still staying with them," Aunt Grace said.

"You chose to believe it," Nick said. "Just as you choose to believe I mean to hurt your niece in some way. I'm not responsible for your beliefs, Miss Winslow, any more than you're responsible for mine."

"I am responsible for my niece, though," Grace said. "And that responsibility includes protecting her from the likes of you."

"But you don't know me," Nick said. "You know nothing about me except what I've told you, and possibly what Mrs. Sinclair said."

"Exactly," Aunt Grace declared. "I know nothing about you, and frankly, I'd be much happier if I could keep it that way. It wouldn't surprise me to learn you'd be happier as well. Shall we strike a bargain, then? You leave Eastgate, forget all about Margaret, and in return, I'll forget this entire incident, and make no effort to investigate you and your undoubtedly unsavory past."

"No deal," Nick said. "No bargain. I couldn't forget Daisy even if I wanted to."

"Very well," Aunt Grace said. "Your past will be an open book to me before I'll allow you to see my niece again."

"That's not fair, Aunt Grace!" Meg said, and she realized that for once Aunt Grace couldn't accuse her of mumbling. "You can't dictate people's lives like that."

"I have no interest in dictating Mr. Sebastian's life," Grace replied. "And I have every right to control yours,

Margaret. You are my ward, and you will remain my ward for the next five years. It was your choice that you moved here. Before then, Marcus was your guardian, and undoubtedly you could have had much more freedom, many fewer restrictions. I don't doubt that Marcus would allow you to see any sort of trash that washes ashore. But you made it obvious to all of us that you were dissatisfied with Marcus, and you moved in with me. Having done that, you must abide by the rules I establish."

"Fine," Meg said. "I'll move in with Uncle Marcus instead. He won't mind. I've changed since then. I'll fit in this time, and you won't ever have to bother about me again."

"It's too late for that," Grace said. "Marcus and I do not exist merely for your convenience, Margaret. Your father was indulged and spoiled, and you have had a life of indulgence as well, and I can see now it has spoiled you too. You give no thought to how you have disrupted the lives of others. All you care about are your own petty, selfish needs."

"Stop it," Nick said. "I won't have you talking that way to her."

"You have no say in the matter," Grace replied. "Margaret, go to your room, and stay there thinking about your selfish, ungrateful attitude. I suggest you leave, Mr. Sebastian, before I am forced to call the police once again. Clark, thank you very much for protecting my niece. I'm not sure she deserves it, but I am in your debt."

Nobody moved.

"I thought I had made myself clear," Grace said. "Margaret, go upstairs immediately."

"I'll run away," she said.

"Daisy, no," Nick said.

"I will," Meg said. "I'll run away and disappear and then you won't ever have to deal with me and my ingratitude again. Isn't that what you want, Aunt Grace? For me to disappear?"

"I want you to behave like a young lady of your social standing," Aunt Grace replied. "Which does not involve running away, as you so dramatically put it."

"Can't you see you're hurting her?" Nick asked. "Doesn't it bother you? I don't care what you say or do to me, but Daisy deserves so much better. How can you not love her?"

"Love is not at issue here," Aunt Grace said. "Ingratitude is, and irresponsibility. Having heard that sad story of yours this morning, I should think that you would know the gratitude Margaret should feel for me. I took her in when no one else would have her."

"You're the one who should be grateful," Nick said. "Daisy owes you nothing."

"She owes me the roof over her head," Grace replied. "She owes me her schooling, her clothes, her tennis and riding lessons. She owes me respect."

Nick shook his head. "I'd rather have my past than hers," he said. "Daisy, I swear to you, I'll get you away from this as soon as I can. Whatever I have to give up for it, I will."

"I know," Meg said.

"Clark, you offered to throw this man out bodily," Aunt Grace said. "I find I must take you up on that offer."

"All right, Miss Winslow," Clark said, but Nick laughed.

"I'll go on my own," he said. "I wouldn't want Clark to sully his hands. Daisy, do what she tells you, but don't

M.A.S. - 4

let it bother you. She doesn't matter, not now, not in our future."

"Mr. Sebastian!" Aunt Grace shouted.

Nick smiled. "I'll be in touch," he said. "Good day, everyone." He nodded his farewells politely, and left the house as though he'd been a welcomed guest.

"You are never to see that man again, Margaret," Aunt Grace declared.

Meg laughed. She sounded like Nick.

"Go to your room at once, Margaret," Aunt Grace said. "And do not expect to be allowed out anytime today."

"Fine," Meg said. She expected to burst into tears, or at least to feel that awful quivering terror that she always felt when Aunt Grace turned her wrath upon her, but those feelings were gone. She had Nick now, and whether he was by her side or not, he enveloped her with his love. He protected her.

CHAPTER SIX

Meg Sebastian

Daisy Sebastian

Margaret Sebastian

Margaret Winslow Sebastian

Margaret Louise Winslow Sebastian

Meg Keefer

Even before Meg heard the footsteps approaching her room, she tore up the list. Not only would Aunt Grace kill her for pairing her name next to Nick's in so many splendid combinations, but Nick, she knew, would be devastated if he saw her name next to Keefer. She wondered if he would love her any the less when he found out her middle name was Louise. But if she could live with George, he could live with Louise. It was Keefer that was the trouble spot.

Meg wished she had matches in her room to burn the names with, but none were allowed her, so she tore the paper into a hundred tiny pieces and scattered them in her wastepaper basket. The servants would never bother to piece the shreds together. She didn't doubt they were under instructions to go through her garbage, but not even Aunt Grace would expect them to paste together such tiny pieces. Even so, she wished she had matches.

It had been two days since she'd seen Nick, two days, four hours, and twelve minutes. She was sure he was counting the days and hours as well, but what else had he done during that time? Was he still at the inn, or had he moved to a boardinghouse? Maybe he'd made up with the Sinclairs, given them flowers and convincing speeches, as he'd given Aunt Grace. Meg knew Caroline Sinclair well enough to know she'd provide little resistance to an attack of charm.

Or had Nick left Eastgate altogether, gone back to Princeton to wait out the summer, or moved on to some other summer resort or returned to wherever he was from, gone back to being George Keefer, given up on Meg, on all his dreams? The uncertainty hurt.

She heard the footsteps then, checked the wastepaper basket to make sure no offending names were visible, and waited for the sound of the key in the lock that now signified social contact for her. With the arrival of the locksmith two days earlier, Meg had lost not only her freedom, but the courtesy of having her door knocked on before entry. All the year-rounders must know that she was being kept locked in her bedroom. It had to be the talk of Eastgate. Were they amused or appalled or did they just regard it as another example of the eccentricities of the rich? Meg wasn't even sure how she felt about it.

Aunt Grace opened the door and stared in at Meg, presumably to confirm that she hadn't escaped. "Clark is here to see you," she declared, and sure enough, she half pushed Clark into Meg's bedroom. "The door will be kept open for the duration of his visit."

"Yes, Aunt Grace," Meg said. It felt funny to speak, even those few words.

"Very well," Aunt Grace said, although Meg knew she didn't think any of this was very well at all. Clark certainly didn't. He appeared terrified. Meg tried not to smile at either of them.

"She has you locked in?" Clark said, as soon as they heard Grace's lumbering footsteps going down the hallway.

Meg nodded. "It's mostly symbolic," she said. "There are no bars on the windows. If I need to escape, I can."

Clark looked out the windows. "You're on the second floor," he pointed out. "What would you do, jump?"

"I haven't worked out the details," Meg replied. "I'm not going to be locked in here forever, Clark. Aunt Grace will come to her senses sooner or later. Why are you here? Did she send for you?"

Clark shook his head. "This was my idea," he said. "Probably a dumb one, too. Mostly I wanted to check up on you. I've been worried. Everyone's been asking where you are. You caused quite a stir at your party, vanishing like that, and then the scene when Nick brought you back, and nobody's seen you since, so everyone's curious."

It hadn't occurred to Meg to think about societal response to her situation. The year-rounders had crossed her mind, but not all the people she'd grown up with. She knew that meant she'd crossed a line, one so natural that she hadn't even been aware of it.

"Are you sure you're all right?" Clark asked.

"I'm fine," Meg said. "I'm getting my three meals a day. I just have to eat them in here."

"You must be bored," Clark said.

"I think about Nicky," Meg replied.

Clark rolled his eyes. "I don't know what's worse," he said. "The way he calls you Daisy or the way you call him Nicky."

Meg was afraid if she laughed Aunt Grace would hear her, so she managed to keep it to a soft giggle. Clark wasn't as concerned, so he laughed outright.

"This is a hell of a situation you've gotten yourself into," Clark said. "Do you have any idea when Grace is going to spring you?"

Meg looked out the window to the ocean. She liked the way it kept its steady rhythm of waves, regardless of what was happening to her. "She said at first I'd have to stay in my room until I was willing to apologize. Which I'm not, and never will be. So I figure that means forever, or until I turn twenty-one."

"That's crazy," Clark said. "She'll have to let you go to school."

"She'll let me out before then," Meg declared. "If people are talking, she isn't going to keep me here all summer. She'll probably free me tomorrow. Your coming here is a good sign."

"That's me all right," Clark said. "Good-Sign Bradford."

"Clark, I'm sorry," Meg said. "I really would like to love you."

Clark almost smiled.

"So," Meg said. "Has anything interesting happened lately? How're Isabelle and her bag boy?"

"They're handling things a lot better than you are," Clark replied. "At least she isn't being held prisoner in her home."

"This isn't my home," Meg said. "This is where I stay summers. I don't have a home, not yet. I haven't since my parents died, and I won't until Nicky and I are together."

"All right," Clark said. "It was a natural mistake on my part."

"I'm sorry," Meg said. "When you're locked in a room for a couple of days, it gives you a chance to think." She giggled. "That's about all it gives you the chance to do. Think and look out windows and write thank-you notes. So what I've been thinking about is who I am, and what my life's been and what it's going to be."

"And your conclusions?" Clark asked.

"That my life is with Nicky," Meg said. "All right, Nick. Does that make you feel better?"

"Not in the slightest," Clark said.

"Have you seen him?" Meg asked.

Clark shook his head. "But I'm willing to if you want," he said so softly Meg almost accused him of mumbling.

"You are?" she asked. "For me? Or just to tell him off?"

Clark pulled his chair closer to Meg's, and bent over to whisper. "I don't like any of this," he said.

"You think I do?" Meg replied.

"And I don't like this new attitude of yours either," Clark said. "If you keep it up, I'll start sympathizing with Grace."

"Prison makes a woman tough," Meg said. "You know, in a funny way, it really does. You should read my thank-you notes. Aunt Grace made me rewrite half of them."

"Are you through?" Clark asked. Meg nodded. "You're not the only one who's been thinking," he said. "I've been thinking too, about you and about Sebastian."

Poor Clark, Meg thought. Who thinks about him?

"And I've come to offer my help," Clark said.

"What?" Meg asked, her voice so loud and filled with surprise half of Eastgate probably heard her.

"Shush," Clark said. "This isn't going to work if you shout about it."

"You really want to help?" Meg asked in tones that matched Clark's.

"Of course I don't want to," Clark said. "But I think you're getting a bum deal. Not just you. Sebastian also. He hasn't committed any crime that I can see, except to claim he's fallen in love with you, and for all I know he has. I can understand why he would." He paused for a moment. "But that's neither here nor there."

"I still don't see why you changed your mind about him," Meg said. "Especially if you haven't gotten to know him."

"I'll tell you why, if you promise you won't think I'm a fool," Clark said. "It was the way he stood up to Grace. Oh, not just the threats to call in the police. I'm sure he's had his share of run-ins with the law, knows how to handle himself in those situations. But he wouldn't let Grace bully you. I love you, but I don't have that kind of courage. Not against Grace Winslow. Maybe because he's an outsider, he just doesn't know any better. Or maybe he really does love you, the way you both seem to think he does. Whatever, I have to admire him. Besides, I feel like a jerk thinking about how I refused to shake his hand."

"You're not a jerk," Meg said. "You're wonderful."

"I know," he said. "I'm the second most wonderful person in the world. So what can I do to help?"

"You can find Nicky for me," Meg replied. "He said

he'd moved into an inn, but that he wouldn't be staying there more than a day. He was going to find a boarding-house with cheaper rents. He doesn't have much money, Clark."

"That is not a selling point in my eyes," Clark said. "But go on."

"I know he needs to see me," Meg said. "And he's probably heard horrible rumors already. You can tell him I'm all right, that I'm thinking about him night and day."

"Hold on," Clark said. "I can live with being a conspirator, but I'm damned if I'm going to be a walking love letter. How's this? If I find him, and I'm not saying I'll be able to, I'll bring him over here tonight."

Meg shook her head. "If Aunt Grace sees him, she really will have him arrested," she replied. "She's been checking up on me at ten-thirty, telling me to turn my lights off. Then at two o'clock, one of the maids has been unlocking the door to make sure I haven't run away. If you could find Nicky, and get a ladder here around midnight, I could slip out, see him in town, and then get back here without anybody knowing."

"Once," Clark said. "I'll do it for you once."

"You won't have to more than once," Meg promised. "Oh Clark, thank you."

"We'll probably all be arrested," Clark said. "Do you know where I'm supposed to find this ladder?"

"There's one in the gardener's shed," Meg said. "It isn't a very tall ladder, but it'll reach high enough."

"Name your firstborn for me," Clark said. "And don't ever tell anybody I was part of this madness."

"Only my firstborn," Meg said. "He'll grow up on the legend of his brave uncle Clark."

"Right," Clark said. "I probably should get out of

here before Grace locks me in. Expect me around midnight, but only if I track Sebastian down. I'm not sticking my neck out for nothing."

"Clark, thank you," Meg said. She stood up, and watched as he left the room. Moments later, Aunt Grace entered.

"Did you have a pleasant visit?" she asked.

"Very nice, Aunt Grace," Meg said. "Thank you for your kindness."

"Are you willing to apologize now?" Grace asked.

"What if I were?" Meg asked.

"You are clearly not yet repentant," Aunt Grace said. "I'm not surprised, although I admit to a certain disappointment. I had hoped for better from you, Margaret. You are, after all, a Winslow."

Meg didn't feel the least bit shriveled.

"I've hired a reputable firm of private investigators," Aunt Grace announced. "Eliot Howe has employed them for his law practice. They have been instructed to find out everything they can about Mr. Sebastian."

"Then what?" Meg asked.

"The chances are excellent they will uncover some criminal activity," Aunt Grace said. "In which case I shall report him to the authorities. Perhaps he is a Communist. Young men with no breeding or character frequently are. There may be grounds for deportation."

"He goes to Princeton," Meg said.

"That proves nothing," Aunt Grace replied. "Princeton is a fine school, but it's located in New Jersey. When I have had a chance to peruse the report, I shall give it to you to read. It should provide the shock you need to come to your senses. Once you discover what this man truly is, you will turn to me in gratitude for saving you from him. Then we shall discuss what the appropriate punishment should be for your arrogant and willful behavior."

"You mean being locked up like this isn't my punishment?" Meg asked.

"Of course not," Aunt Grace declared. "It is for your protection."

"My protection from what?" Meg asked.

"From Mr. Sebastian," Aunt Grace replied. "And from your own baser instincts."

"I love him," Meg said, although she knew that made no difference. "And there's a real chance I'm stuck with my baser instincts for life."

"With willpower and sacrifice, we may rise above our very natures," Aunt Grace declared. "But it is always wise to protect a child. When I agreed to take you in, I was warned that your behavior might prove irrational. Institutionalization was suggested then. Marcus, I must tell you, was firmly in favor, but I felt there was no need for such public humiliation. A young girl who has been labeled mentally ill cannot possibly assume her rightful place in society. Think about that, Margaret, while you sit in your pretty room. Think about all you're risking for this unworthy young man."

"You wouldn't," Meg said.

"Your mother was flighty and unstable," Grace said. "But Reggie would have her, and he paid for that folly with his life. It would come as a surprise to no one if their daughter was also marked by such character flaws. You are my ward, Margaret, and if I feel the only way you can be saved from yourself is by being kept in an institution, I will do it gladly."

"But I'm not crazy," Meg said. "You know I'm not. Let me talk to Uncle Marcus. I can convince him."

"I have already spoken with him," Grace replied. "He agrees that I know what is best for you. Indeed, at his urging, I have contacted a sanitarium he knows of, and made plans to have you sent there, should it prove necessary. But I'm confident that the detective's report will shock you to your senses, and that following an appropriate punishment, and a change of schools, you will return to your previous wholesome self."

"Change of schools?" Meg asked. Her future was whirling past her, and there was no Nick, no hope.

"That has already been arranged for," Grace said. "An Anglican convent school in Surrey. A school known for its strictness. I will escort you to England at the end of August, and stay on in Europe for a few months. Perhaps if you have proven yourself worthy, we will be able to spend Christmas together in London. If not, you will remain in the school until the sisters feel you have earned the right to outside contact."

"So what you're offering me is a choice of prisons," Meg said. She stared out the window to the ocean. It was no longer her ally.

"Look at me when we're speaking," Aunt Grace said. "It is such a small courtesy, and you owe me that."

"I'm sorry," Meg said. "It hurts me to look at you."

"How do you think I feel?" Grace demanded. "To look at Reggie's only child and see a girl yearning to throw herself into the abyss."

"I'm sorry," Meg said. "I wish for your sake I didn't have feelings."

"You will learn to overcome them," Grace said. "You are already learning that life is more than birthday parties and sugared sweets. In the long run, this little misadventure may prove helpful. Two years in a convent school, spending your days in education and prayer, may give you the discipline that appears to be lacking in your nature. And when you graduate, you will return to Boston, with all hints of scandal long forgotten, and be able to make your debut as proudly and rightly as any of your friends. No doubt some young man from a proper family will be willing to overlook this summertime indiscretion, and you'll make an appropriate marriage. That is all we hope for, Marcus and I. That your life turn out exactly as it is meant to."

"What happens between now and August?" Meg asked. "There's what, five or six weeks before we would have to go?"

"That depends exclusively on you," Aunt Grace replied. "Unfortunately, I cannot trust you in your current emotional state, so you will remain in your room until the detective's report has arrived."

"But that could be months," Meg said.

"Mr. Sebastian is a very young man," Aunt Grace said. "He cannot have committed an endless stream of crimes. The agency promised me results in ten days to two weeks."

"And what if the report shows nothing?" Meg asked. There was always the chance, after all, that they wouldn't be able to turn up Nick's illegitimacy, or that Aunt Grace wouldn't care, just as long as he wasn't an ax murderer.

"Then we shall both be very surprised," Grace said.

"That's not fair," Meg said, wanting some kind of concession on Grace's part, whether it was likely or not. "If the report shows that Nick is exactly who he says he is, an orphaned student at Princeton with all those A's, then I think you'll owe him and me an apology."

"I would not provoke me any further if I were you, Margaret," Aunt Grace declared. "Such behavior suggests mental instability."

"I'm sorry," Meg said. She wondered how many apologies she had in her, and how many it might take to keep from being put in a sanitarium. Two of the girls she knew at school had mothers who had been locked up years before, and there was never any talk of their being released. Aunt Grace wasn't one for idle threats. Meg knew the risk was real.

"Following the reading of the report, you will have two courses of action available to you," Aunt Grace said. "The first, and proper one, will be to acknowledge that I was right in protecting you from the danger that Mr. Sebastian represents. You will agree to whatever punishment Marcus and I decide upon, and then go willingly with me to England to begin your two years at the convent school."

"Don't get me wrong," Meg said. "But what kind of punishment are you thinking of?"

There was a flicker of a smile on Aunt Grace's face. "Nothing horrendous," she said. "Your removal from Eastgate, perhaps. A carefully supervised summer on Beacon Hill instead."

Prison again, Meg thought, but she doubted Grace would mar her Boston mansion with locks.

"Or perhaps we will permit you to stay on at Eastgate, but severely limit your social activities," Aunt Grace continued. "You would not be allowed out evenings, nor could you have any friends over."

"Not even Clark?" Meg asked.

"An exception might be made for Clark, if his parents are willing," Grace said. "His father has already expressed concern to me about your behavior. He doesn't want you to corrupt Clark in any way."

"Clark is incorruptible," Meg said.

"The same might once have been said of you," Aunt Grace replied. "Marcus and I have made no firm decisions, nor will we until we determine what your attitude is. But whatever we'll decide, it will be for your welfare."

"What if . . ." Meg began, and then she cleared her throat. She knew what she was about to ask was a mistake, but somehow it felt important that she not lie any more than she had to to Aunt Grace. Meg believed in honor and in honesty, and wanted to claim for herself that incorruptible core she knew remained in her. "What if I read the detective's report, and no matter what's in it, it doesn't make any difference in how I feel?"

"The sanitarium is on twenty-four hours' alert," Aunt Grace replied. "They will provide an ambulance, so you will have no chance to escape."

"Would you keep me there forever?" Meg asked. "Just because I love Nicky?"

"This love, as you call it, is nothing more than a symptom," Aunt Grace said. "A symptom of a deep psychological disturbance. Once you get the help you need, you will undoubtedly make a full recovery. You are a Winslow, after all, and Winslows are healthy and mentally sound. This sickness of yours must come from your mother's side, and since she came from a good family as well, I'm sure you will be able to assume some sort of limited role in society, in years to come."

"This is so unfair," Meg said.

"Unfair for whom?" Aunt Grace said. "I'm sure I've given you a great deal to think about, so I'll leave you now. You are a good girl, Margaret, or at least you once were, and I'm sure once you come to your senses, you will be again. I want no foolishness from you during the next few days. Spend them in thought and in prayer, and you will undoubtedly see the error of your ways."

"Yes, Aunt Grace," Meg said. She rose as Grace left the room, then sat down and listened while the door was relocked. The sound was no longer amusing to her. There might well be a lifetime of locks to deal with, endless days and nights of imprisonment.

She paced around the room, feeling trapped, until she realized she had felt trapped since her parents had died, trapped at Uncle Marcus's, trapped at Aunt Grace's, trapped even at school. It was only when she was with Nick that she felt free.

Nick would rescue her. If Aunt Grace wanted Meg to pray, then pray she would. She closed her eyes and prayed for Clark, for a ladder, for Nick's arms around her, for the freedom to love, to feel.

CHAPTER SEVEN

At precisely seven minutes after twelve, the ladder materialized under Meg's window.

The day had been a nightmare, but it was nothing compared to the slow torture Meg had endured between ten-thirty and midnight. Aunt Grace had entered Meg's room at bedtime, insisted on a proper good-night, and seen to it that all lights were off and Meg was in bed. Naturally, as soon as Grace left, Meg climbed out of bed, but without any light, there was nothing she could do in the room except sit, wait, think, and watch the luminous dial on her clock move with excruciating slowness. Meg knew Clark might not show up with the ladder. She knew he might come some other night, or not at all. There were a thousand reasons not to count on Clark, but she counted on him anyway. Clark was the road to her salvation, and he knew it. He'd never let her down before. Granted, she'd never asked very much of him, but he'd always been there for the little things, and now he had to be there for the big ones as well.

Meg listened during that hour and a half as the house was put to sleep. Aunt Grace went to bed at eleven each night, and she didn't like the servants rumbling about, so they were in their rooms within a half hour. The house was dark and still, as was the night. It felt to Meg as though she were the only person conscious of the air.

And then the ladder appeared, and Clark at the foot of it, gesturing frantically for Meg to come down. Meg had tossed on the skirt and blouse she intended to wear the next day, but she wore her sneakers instead of her usual loafers. Aunt Grace hated those sneakers, and just putting them on felt like an act of rebellion.

The window was open, and all Meg had to do was unlatch the bottom of the screen and climb out carefully onto the ladder. She knew under different circumstances she would have been terrified to get on that ladder, climb down the rungs in almost total darkness. The Meg she had been just a few days earlier never would have had the courage. Who knew what the Meg she was becoming might have the strength to do.

Clark gestured her to remain quiet, so she kept her thoughts to herself as they hid the ladder behind some trees. They maintained their silence until they were a safe distance from the house.

"Did you find Nicky?" Meg asked.

Clark shook his head. "What do you think?" he asked. "I risked life and limb and the wrath of Grace Winslow just to see you on ground level? You're not the only one who could get into trouble because of this little caper, you know. My father would have my head if he ever found out."

"You're right, and I'm sorry," Meg said. "I should have thanked you right away. I'm very grateful, Clark."

"That's better," he said. "And yes, I found your precious Nicky."

"Where is he?" Meg asked. "Is he all right?"

"He's on our stretch of beach," Clark replied. "We both thought it might be safer there. Do you have any idea what you asked of me, Meg? I had to go through some unsavory parts of town to locate that boardinghouse he's moved to. And then it took me close to an hour to convince him I wasn't the enemy, and my offer was on the level. He thought it was some kind of trap. Nick Sebastian is a very suspicious man."

"But you did convince him," Meg said. "And he's really waiting for me."

"If he hasn't caught cold," Clark said. "You would pick a rainy night for this rendezvous."

"It's only misting," Meg said. "You have no idea how good the rain feels on my arms."

"Is it awful being locked up?" Clark asked. "I had the measles once when I was a kid, and I wasn't allowed out of my room for a couple of weeks, but it was wintertime, and I don't remember minding. It must be different in the summer. And of course you aren't sick."

Meg wished Clark would keep quiet and just let her enjoy the air and the anticipation of seeing Nick. He's really there, she thought. He's really waiting for me.

"He's not a bad sort when you talk with him," Clark said. "That boardinghouse he's staying in is appalling. I didn't know they let those sorts of people into Eastgate. We've led very sheltered lives, Meg. I hope you realize that. We've been protected from the worst society has to offer."

"And Nick hasn't?" Meg asked.

"There's a hardness to him you may not see," Clark

replied. "He tried to hide it from me, but it came through with all his questions. But his facade really is quite charming. And he's obviously well-read. As far as I could see, his only possessions were books."

"I'm sure he has a nicer room at Princeton," Meg said. She thought she spotted him on the beach, but it was just some driftwood.

"Rooms at Princeton are all right," Clark replied. He was going to Dartmouth himself. "Meg, don't let him hurt you."

"He won't," Meg said. "I know you're worried, and I really do appreciate it, Clark, but it isn't necessary."

"That's a matter of opinion," Clark replied.

Meg sighed. "I know I owe you a thousand thank-yous," she said. "And a couple of massive favors. Whatever you want, I'll do."

"Just marry me once you're finished with Sebastian," Clark said. "Or he's finished with you, which'll probably happen first."

"Why do you say that?" Meg asked. Had Nick tired of her already? Was that what Clark was trying to tell her?

"I'm sure he's after you for your money," Clark said. "Once he gets his hands on it, he'll be gone."

Meg laughed with relief. "You're wrong," she said. "Someday you'll realize that."

"I hope I am wrong," Clark said. "But I'll stick around just in case I'm not."

"You won't stick around tonight, though," Meg said, trying to keep the anxiety out of her voice. "You'll leave us alone, won't you?"

"I intend to stay close by," Clark replied. "To see to it you're safe. What do you really know about him, Meg?

He could be a rapist or a murderer, and then where would I be?"

"In better shape than me," Meg said, but she knew Clark would never give way on this issue. "You can watch us, if it makes you feel better, but we need privacy to talk. You have to give us that." She longed for the day when she could stop begging.

"All right," Clark said. "But I'll be in earshot if you start screaming."

"Thank you," Meg said. She turned to kiss Clark on the cheek, but then she saw Nick, and she ran toward him.

Nick spotted her at the same time, and he raced to her side as well. They were together, embracing, within seconds. Clark, alas, was there moments later.

"I've already told Meg," he said. "I'm going to be standing right over there, watching you, the entire time you're together. So don't get any ideas, Sebastian."

"Fine," Nick said. "All right. Whatever you say." He smiled at Meg, who lost herself in his happiness.

"Right over there," Clark said, pointing to a spot a couple of hundred feet away. When he decided his point had been made, he walked away from them, then stood at conspicuous attention on the designated location.

Nick and Meg embraced again, and then kissed. The kiss convinced Meg that somehow, everything would work out.

"I was so afraid I'd never see you again," Meg whispered. "Hold me, Nicky. Don't let me go."

"I was a fool," Nick said. "A fool and a coward. I should have just gone to your aunt, demanded to see you."

"No," Meg said. "That would have been the worst

thing you could have done. Are you all right? Clark says you're in an awful boardinghouse."

Nick laughed. "I've been in worse," he said. "I don't think Clark is much of a connoisseur of boardinghouses."

"I wish I could be there with you," Meg said.

"Clark says she's keeping you locked up," Nick said. "Is that true?"

"It's true enough," Meg replied. "But I'm here with you now."

"Has she hurt you?" Nick asked.

It took Meg a moment to realize what he was asking. "She hasn't hit me," she said. "Aunt Grace doesn't hit. She doesn't even ask her servants to hit."

"I didn't know," Nick said. "I was scared. I kept picturing her striking you."

"That will never happen," Meg said. "Don't ever worry about that again."

Nick kissed her. "I've wanted you so much," he said.

"I know," Meg said. "All I think about is you. I was so afraid you'd left Eastgate, but I kept hoping maybe the Sinclairs had decided to invite you back. Have you spoken to them?"

Nick laughed harshly. Meg wondered if she'd ever be able to remove the pain from that sound. "Mrs. Sinclair paid me a call," he said. "She suggested that if I was no longer interested in her daughter, perhaps I could move back in and show some interest in her instead."

"Did she really?" Meg asked. She knew Nick was beautiful, but she'd never thought to worry that somebody's mother might think so as well.

"It was no big deal," Nick replied. "I've had offers like that before. I turned her down politely, but I doubt she'll have many nice things to say about me. I guess I won't be seeing much of Robert back at Princeton."

For the moment, Meg didn't care about Robert Sinclair. "Do you always turn those offers down?" she asked. "All the ones from older women?"

"I've turned them down," Nick said. "I'm not a gigolo, Daisy. And Grace isn't a child beater. We've both learned something today."

"I love you," Meg said. "I can't believe I've been standing here talking with you for five minutes already, and I hadn't even remembered to tell you that."

"You've shown me," Nick said. "You are a miracle, Daisy. Do you have any idea how wonderful you are?"

"No," Meg admitted. "I can't get over the idea that you love me. You do love me, don't you, Nicky?"

"Now and forever," Nick said, and they kissed to prove it.

Meg laughed softly in the mist. "We're some pair," she said. "Do you think we'll ever get used to the idea of each other?"

"I don't think so," Nick replied. "I don't see how I can ever get used to happiness."

"I know," Meg said. "I was dead before I met you. I went through the motions, did all the things I was supposed to do, but inside me there was nothing. Just a residue of fear. Then there you were, and suddenly I could feel again, joy and excitement. Hold on to me, Nicky. Don't ever let me go."

"I love you," Nick said. "And somehow or another, we'll work things out, and I'll see to it that you're always happy. You deserve so much, Daisy. All the happiness there is in this world."

"We'll share it," Meg said. "Oh Nicky, I wish I could

hold on to you like this forever. Well, maybe not in the rain." She laughed softly with the joy of being in his arms.

"How much time do we have?" Nick asked.

"Not much," Meg replied. "I have to be back by two, but I don't think Clark will let me stay that long. He's worried, and he's right to be, and I've imposed on him so much already. We have to talk, Nicky. We have to work things out."

Nick nodded. "What's going on?" he asked. "Has Grace given you any idea of when she's going to free you?"

"This is complicated," Meg said. "She hired detectives to write a report on you. It should be delivered in ten days or so. She's hoping I'll read it, and be so shocked I'll come to my senses. Then I'm supposed to beg her forgiveness, and show her my gratitude for the way she kept me from destroying my life."

"Why do bullies always expect gratitude?" Nick asked. "I used to wonder about that with my stepfather."

"I guess they feel if we're grateful, it means they're right," Meg said. "But Aunt Grace really isn't nearly as bad as your stepfather."

"That doesn't sound too bad," Nick declared. "You read the report, and then you act the way she wants you to. I'm a cad and she's a saint. If you can fool her, she'll give you your freedom, and then somehow we'll manage to see each other."

Meg knew Nick was right, but she didn't care for his attitude anyway. "Is there anything in that report I won't know about?" she asked. "Anything I really will be shocked over?"

Nick thought for a moment. "I'm sure there won't

be," he said. "Grace is going to hate it that I'm a bastard. No, that isn't true. She'll love it. Her only disappointment will be that my father is a banker, and not a sailor or a lumberjack."

"He's a banker?" Meg asked.

"Very respectable," Nick replied. "What did your father do?"

"He went through his inheritance," Meg said. "That's why I don't have any money."

"Was he happy?" Nick asked.

"Oh yes," Meg replied. "He was very happy."

"Then he did the right thing," Nick said. "We'll work things out. I'll stay on in Eastgate, and we'll find a way to see each other. It should be easier once the school year starts. Girls can always find ways to slip out of boarding schools."

Meg shook her head. "There's more," she said. "And it's going to make you angry. You have to promise you won't get too upset, no matter what I tell you."

"I don't know," Nick replied. "What are you going to tell me?"

Meg tried to smile. "There's bad news, and there's worse news," she said. "The bad news is, I'm not going back to Miss Arnold's. They're sending me to a boarding school in England instead. It sounds like it has twelve-foot walls and barbed-wire windows, and I'll be there for the next two years. If I behave myself, they may let me out for vacations."

"England," Nick said. "Well, that isn't surprising. They figure if they put some distance between us, we'll fall apart. Maybe I can spend my junior year abroad, if I can get the money together."

"That might hurt worse," Meg said. "Knowing you

H.A.S. - 5

were in the same country, and we couldn't even see each other. I don't know. It's not for another year yet anyway."

"You said that was the bad part," Nick said. "What could be worse?"

Meg stared out at the ocean. She knew she couldn't face Nick and tell him. "She's threatening to put me in a sanitarium," she whispered. It hurt too much to say the words out loud, even with just Nick and the sea gulls to hear her.

"What?" Nick said.

The mist had turned into a soft but steady rain. Meg felt the drops mingle with her tears. "She's worried that I'm crazy," she said. "I think it's more Uncle Marcus's idea. It's all arranged, though. They're on twenty-four-hour alert if they're needed."

"They would do that to you?" Nick asked. "Just because you love me?"

Meg nodded. "They don't understand," she said. "They don't know you. You scare them somehow."

"You're the one who scares them," Nick replied. "Because you have feelings. They're not used to that, and it frightens them. Oh Daisy, what have I done to you."

"You've given me life," Meg said. "You've loved me."

"That isn't enough," Nick said. "You're wrong, Daisy. They are worse than my stepfather. I swear to you, if they even try to have you committed, I'll kill them. I'll see them dead before they do that to you."

Meg knew Nick meant it, and it terrified her. What had she done to him? What was he willing to risk for her love?

"It'll be all right," she said. "I think it's just a threat so I won't make too big a fuss over the new school. There'd be a scandal if I were put away. Too many people would know and talk about it. They hate that. When my parents died, well, it wasn't their fault, but there was a lot of talk, and Uncle Marcus and Aunt Grace hated it. They just want me to be afraid."

Nick kissed her. "You're the bravest person I know," he said. "They're fools to think they can break you."

"They don't want to break me," Meg said. "Not the way you mean. They want me to be someone I'm not, and they don't know how to make me into that person, so they're trying all kinds of crazy things. They'd say they're just trying to protect me, and they'd mean it, too."

"You're too kind to them," Nick said. "They don't deserve you." He laughed. "But then again, neither do I. All right. She shows you the report, and you act all horrified, and then we take it from there. Can you do that? It almost makes me wish I hadn't been honest with you, so you really might be upset. You're the first person I've ever been honest with. Maybe I was wrong."

"Shush," Meg said. "You were right. I love you, and I don't need your pretty stories. I hate the thought of pretending, but if that's what I have to do, then I'll do it."

"It's only for a couple of years," Nick said. "Once you're eighteen, we can be together."

"Do we have to wait that long?" Meg asked. She clenched her hands into fists and forced herself to be as brave as Nick thought she was. "In my room tonight, well, I had nothing else to do except think, so I thought a lot, and it occurred to me, we could elope right now. Well, not this very minute, because Clark would never let us, but in a few days. You could help me escape, and we could go to some state where sixteen-year-olds can get married without parental consent, and then Aunt Grace couldn't do anything, like send me away to school, or put me in a sanitarium, because I'd be your wife. I'd quit school and get a job, and you could finish college. I know it wouldn't be Princeton, but at least we'd be together. Couldn't we, Nicky? Couldn't we do that?"

"You'd give up everything like that?" Nick asked. "Just for me?"

"I have nothing to give up," Meg said.

"That isn't true," Nick declared. "You have a lot. They just don't seem important to you right now, but you have family and friends and social position and money. You'd be giving all that up for me."

"Gladly," Meg said. "Please, Nicky. Please say yes."

Nick shook his head. "It seems like the right thing to do tonight, in the rain," he said. "But tomorrow morning, you may not think so. We don't have to decide tonight. Maybe things will work out for us some other way. Maybe Grace will come to her senses, realize she's risking losing you. Let's just see how it goes before we decide on anything."

Meg knew Nick was right, but she felt disappointed anyway. Nick saw it in her face, and kissed her. "I love you," he said. "And I want you, and I want to be your husband. Don't doubt that, Daisy. Don't ever doubt that."

"I won't," she said, and felt relieved and happy in his arms. "Kiss me again, and then I should go."

Nick nodded. They shared one last kiss, and then Meg forced herself to walk away from him, toward Clark. She wanted to turn around and stare at Nick, but she was afraid she'd never leave if she did, so she kept her back to him and thought only about how safe she felt with him, how loved, how happy.

Clark had the kindness not to speak until they were far away from Nick. "Do you feel better?" he asked then. "Was it worth the risk?"

"Much better," Meg said. "He loves me."

"That's not hard to do," Clark said.

Meg smiled. "We even talked about getting married," she said. "Now, this summer, if we have to."

"You're a fool," Clark said, and he kept quiet for the rest of the walk back to Grace's, back to the locked room.

CHAPTER EIGHT

"Come, Margaret. We don't want to be late."

"No, Aunt Grace," Meg replied, and picked up her pace. She'd been walking slowly on purpose, so Aunt Grace wouldn't see how excited she was to be let out of the house. But if Aunt Grace wanted speed, then speed she'd get.

"There's no need for you to run," Aunt Grace promptly declared. "We're going to church, not the racetrack. Take ladylike steps, Margaret."

"Yes, Aunt Grace," Meg said, trying to match her steps to Grace's. She hadn't been running or anything close to it, so it was wrong of Aunt Grace to claim she had. Maybe all those years Grace had accused her of mumbling and stooping, Meg hadn't mumbled or stooped even once. It was a heady thought.

"I trust you will behave yourself," Aunt Grace said as they climbed into the car that would drive them the mile or so to church.

"Yes, Aunt Grace," Meg said. She'd managed her midnight tryst with Nick, and had for the two days since then been a model prisoner, always polite, never rebellious. Sunday had finally arrived, and with it, an outing to church, and then who knew what wonderful new freedoms. Meg refused to believe she'd be locked up again, at least not on the Sabbath.

It felt great to be in a car moving anywhere, even if the distance was short and the company unpleasant. Meg stared out the window, saw the people she'd grown up with as they too approached their house of worship. The weather was perfect, sunny and in the eighties. Meg wondered if she might be able to convince Grace to let her have a walk around the garden once they got home. She knew better than to ask for swimming privileges, but Grace might have it in her heart to agree to a short, well-supervised stroll. Meg pictured plunging a dagger into that shriveled heart, and giggled with pleasure at the image.

"I fail to see what's humorous," Aunt Grace said. "Do you intend to laugh like a hyena throughout the service?"

Probably, Meg thought, but she shook her head and tried to look somber. You're an old woman, she said to Grace silently, and I'm young and in love and that terrifies you. She tried picturing Aunt Grace young, and even though she'd seen many photographs of her in her teens, she couldn't imagine it.

"People may ask questions," Aunt Grace said. "You will know better than to answer them."

"Yes, Aunt Grace," Meg said.

"Very well," Grace said. "Stay by my side at all

times, and remember, this is a church service, and not some picnic event for you to run wild at."

Meg nodded. She followed Grace out of the car, and to their pew at the church. She saw all the familiar faces there, and was certain she was being stared at. Everyone in town must know what's going on, she decided, and Aunt Grace is probably embarrassed. Maybe even ashamed that she has a niece capable of falling in love in such a spectacular fashion. Meg's dress was navy blue, conservative and completely acceptable, but she felt as though she were wearing scarlet. She began to blush, and could feel herself shaking.

"Stop making a spectacle of yourself," Aunt Grace whispered, and grabbing Meg's arm, pulled her to their seats. Meg pushed her imaginary dagger deeper into Grace, then thought how inappropriate the thought was inside a church, and blushed all the harder.

"Sit down," Aunt Grace whispered, and gave Meg a push. Meg sat. She looked down, trying to keep from crying. She'd been looking forward to this trip for days, and now Aunt Grace was turning it into another nightmare. She could hear the whispers around her, and she was sure she made out the word "unstable" from a row or two behind her.

Then suddenly she thought, Maybe Nicky is here. The church was a public place, after all, and while she and Nick had never discussed religion, she was sure he was some sort of compatible denomination, and would feel perfectly at ease in her church. The idea that he was there, under the same roof, made her look up and around, but there was no Nick.

"Stop gawking," Aunt Grace said. "You're acting like a tourist."

Meg began to lower her head, but before she completely sank into embarrassed oblivion, she caught a glimpse of Clark, who smiled at her. She smiled back. At least she had one friend there. That was more than Aunt Grace had.

The service, which usually dragged for Meg, went entirely too fast. Meg was certain that her behavior had made Grace decide to lock her back up as soon as they got home, all that running and blushing and gawking, just the kinds of things Grace hated. Meg pictured Grace slipping handcuffs on her, but she didn't even smile. No freedom, no Nick, no smiles.

After the service, Grace stood around with Meg by her side, and said hello to various people, almost as though it were an average Sunday morning. Nobody said anything to them about Meg's peculiar behavior of late, and Grace certainly didn't bring it up. Meg thought about making a break for it, running away on that beautiful July morning, vanishing into the netherworlds of Eastgate, finding Nick, finding a new home, but she hardly had the strength to stand there, exposed in public, and she knew she wouldn't make it fifty feet before collapsing into a blushing heap. Awful as it was, it was easier to stand next to Grace and mumble the sorts of things people expected her to mumble. What a pretty day it was. What a stimulating sermon. How good the choir sounded. How lovely her birthday party had been. Mumble and stoop, just the way Grace claimed.

"Come, Margaret," Aunt Grace said, when the socializing time of the day had ended. "It's time to go back home."

"Yes, Aunt Grace," Meg said. She tried to look around

inconspicuously, in case Nick had slipped into the neighborhood, was lurking around in a doorway or behind a tree, waiting for her to see him so he could say, "I love you." But if Nick was there, he was doing too good a job at lurking, and Meg couldn't find him. He probably wasn't there. Meg suspected she'd made him up, that none of this had happened, that Grace had always kept her locked up because of her unstable tendencies.

"You will stay downstairs for dinner," Aunt Grace declared, once they were in the privacy of the car. "Depending on your behavior, I may allow you to spend the rest of the day in the parlor."

Meg wanted to ask if she could walk through the garden, but she lacked the courage. "Thank you, Aunt Grace," she said instead.

"Stop mumbling," Aunt Grace said. "I shall have to see if at St. Bartholomew's they can provide you with speech lessons. You certainly need to learn to enunciate."

"Is that the name of the school?" Meg asked. "St. Bartholomew's?"

"Yes," Grace replied. "It's an excellent school too. Father John mentioned to me yesterday that he knew a young girl several years back who had been an enormous worry to her parents, she drank, he said, and got into trouble with the law, and after three years at St. Bartholomew's, she was able to return to society and behave quite properly."

"What kind of trouble with the law?" Meg asked.

"He wasn't at liberty to tell me," Aunt Grace said. "But I imagine he was talking about the Bishop girl. I know she went to St. Bartholomew's."

Meg tried to remember all she could about Georgina Bishop. "She's married now, isn't she," she said.

"To the Phelps boy," Aunt Grace said. "A fine match. I'm sure she regarded her three years at St. Bartholomew's as a small price to pay for being able to assume her proper role in life."

Meg pictured herself spending two years at St. Bartholomew's, only to graduate into marriage with Clark. If the car had been moving faster, she would have flung herself out of it.

"I spoke to Maude Bishop about St. Bartholomew's," Aunt Grace declared. "While Marcus and I were discussing your alternatives."

"What's it like there?" Meg asked, trying to sound casual without mumbling.

"Of course they're very strict," Aunt Grace said. "That's the whole point of a school of that sort. To provide girls from proper families with a school that offers them sufficient structure to keep them from sordid mistakes."

"Do a lot of Americans go there?" Meg asked.

"My understanding is it's quite an international school," Aunt Grace replied. "It seems there are girls with your sort of behavior problems to be found in many different countries."

"That sounds nice," Meg said, not knowing what she was supposed to say.

Apparently, she'd guessed wrong. Aunt Grace barked with laughter. "It's hardly nice," she said. "To satisfy Marcus, I had to find a school with the strictest of guidelines. There are morning prayers at six, and lights are out by nine. Classes are held six days a week, and the only free time is three hours Sunday afternoons."

"Oh," Meg said. Miss Arnold's was starting to sound like a pleasure palace in comparison.

"The British are quite a bit stricter than Americans," Aunt Grace declared. "I probably should have taken you out of Miss Arnold's when I assumed your custodianship. You obviously need more structure than you'd been receiving there."

The car pulled into the circular driveway, and Grace and Meg entered the house together. Meg wondered how long she'd be allowed to stay downstairs, and whether in a few months' time, her stay at Eastgate would seem like a festival of freedom.

They sat down for dinner soon after they got in. The dining room always seemed empty with just the two of them there, but, as always, Meg was glad for whatever distance the large table provided between her and Grace.

"You mentioned that we might spend Christmas together," Meg said. She knew she was a fool to ask more questions about the school, but it was like an aching tooth that constantly drew the tongue to it. "Are the girls allowed much time away from school?"

Aunt Grace speared a piece of ham from her plate. "Very little," she replied. "And of course, none of it unsupervised. During the first six months, new girls are not allowed to leave the grounds at all, except at Christmas. Thereafter, if their behavior proves them trustworthy, they may go to town in a group, accompanied by two of the sisters, once a month to buy toiletries and the like. In addition, in case you're getting any ideas, they are allowed no visitors outside their immediate families, and any letters they send out or receive are read by the sisters."

"Then they can get letters," Meg said. It was such a small thing, but it was all Grace was leaving her.

"I will give them a list of people you may receive mail

from," Aunt Grace replied. "Nick Sebastian's name will not be on that list."

Meg knew better than to ask about phone calls. For two years, she knew, she wouldn't see Nick, or even hear from him. Two years, and that was the better of the two alternatives Grace was offering her. "What are the rooms like?" she asked instead.

"There are no rooms," Grace declared. "Not the sort you're used to at Miss Arnold's. The girls sleep in dormitories, twenty beds to a room. According to Maude Bishop, Georgina complained about the lack of heat her entire stay there."

Meg wondered how much this hellhole cost, then decided the price was probably quite high. After all, the parents who sent their daughters there could sleep comfortably in their well-heated bedrooms, knowing how cleverly they were punishing their offspring.

"I'm sure I'll learn a lot there," Meg said.

"Yes," Aunt Grace replied. "Undoubtedly you will."

Meg ate as much as she could of her lunch, not wishing to alienate Grace even further by showing a lack of appetite. She thought she could bear anything if she knew that Nick was there for her, but two years of enforced isolation with no chance of seeing him might be more than she could handle. And she knew the risk existed that Nick might not wait for her.

Following lunch, Grace made no mention of Meg returning to her room, so she went instead into the parlor, where she sat doing needlepoint while Grace read. Occasionally she gazed out the window, but Grace didn't take the hint. Meg thought about going to the piano and playing some music appropriate to Sunday afternoon, but she didn't know if that pleasure was also forbidden, and she lacked the courage to find out. Meg could feel Aunt Grace's stare every now and again, but tried hard not to look up, tried harder not to blush. They sat that way for an hour, until the doorbell rang.

Delman had Sundays off, so one of the maids answered the door, and let Clark Bradford and his father in. They were ushered to the parlor, where Grace greeted them.

"I'm pleased to see you both here," Mr. Bradford declared, after sitting down and refusing the offer of lemonade. "I heard some distressing news, that I thought it my place to share with you."

Meg put down her needlepoint and glanced at Clark. He shook his head slightly, and Meg knew it was going to be bad.

"It concerns that Sebastian fellow," Mr. Bradford said. "The one who made such a fuss at Margaret's party."

"Has he committed a crime?" Aunt Grace asked. "Have the police been called in?"

"It's not like that," Clark said, but his father shushed him.

"It's a great deal like that," Mr. Bradford said. "My understanding was you'd made it quite clear to Sebastian that he wasn't welcome in Eastgate."

"I believe he knows that," Aunt Grace said.

"I should have spoken to him," Mr. Bradford said. "I know this is a family matter, and I'm not family, but there are times when a man simply has to step in, and this, I'm afraid, was one of them."

"What happened?" Meg asked. Had Nick been hurt? How badly did he need her?

"I've just come from the club," Mr. Bradford said.

"We decided to have lunch there, then do a bit of sailing. And Sebastian was all people were talking about."

"Not in reference to Margaret?" Grace said, and Meg could hear a layer of panic in her voice.

"Thank heavens no," Mr. Bradford replied. "No, the scandal this time revolves around Sebastian and Caroline Sinclair."

"Mrs. Sinclair?" Meg asked. "What does she have to do with anything?"

"Margaret, be still," Aunt Grace said. "Or I shall have to tell you to leave the room."

"No, don't, she should hear this," Mr. Bradford said. "As I'm sure you've heard, the Sinclairs had invited Sebastian to spend the summer with them, although they hardly knew the boy."

"No one seems to know him well," Aunt Grace said. "I suspect he's a confidence man."

"You may be right," Mr. Bradford said. "In any case, following that ugly scene at Margaret's party, the Sinclairs told him to leave. They expected, as you did, that he would leave Eastgate altogether, move on to some other resort, or else revert to his own social level and get a job waiting tables or caddying. It was no concern of theirs, once Henry and Caroline got Robert to swear he would have no further contact with Sebastian back at Princeton."

"But he didn't leave," Aunt Grace said. "He's still here, I gather."

"Worse even than that," Mr. Bradford declared. "Caroline Sinclair found some of his belongings in her house, and she foolishly decided to return them on her own."

"Caroline Sinclair has a foolish streak," Aunt Grace said. "It's gotten her into trouble over the years."

"It did once again," Mr. Bradford said. "She went to

some wretched boardinghouse Sebastian has holed himself up in, and after she returned his things to him, he grew ugly and made advances."

Aunt Grace sat up even straighter than usual. "I wish I could say I was surprised," she said. "But I could see the animal in him from the start."

"Fortunately, Caroline was able to escape," Mr. Bradford said. "She was quite distraught over the incident. Henry threatened to chase him out of town with a bullwhip, and several of us at the club would have been more than willing to join him."

"Is she pressing charges?" Aunt Grace asked.

Mr. Bradford shook his head. "They want to avoid a scandal," he replied. "To protect Isabelle as much as anything else. But I felt you should know, especially as Sebastian appears to be remaining here, with no sense of shame or decency. I'm afraid he might make some kind of effort to see Margaret again. A man like that could resort to anything, even abduction, to get his way."

"All the more reason to keep Margaret supervised," Aunt Grace said. "In August, of course, I'll be taking her to St. Bartholomew's, and there she'll certainly be safe."

"Until then, or at least until you know that Sebastian has left Eastgate, I recommend keeping Margaret by your side at all times," Mr. Bradford said. "To protect both her and her reputation. I've already heard talk."

"We cannot have that," Aunt Grace agreed, and Meg had a terrible insight. If the talk continued, if Meg developed some sort of reputation, then Clark would be forbidden to see her. Not only would she lose Nick, but she would lose her only real friend in the world.

"You're wrong about him," she said. "Nicky would never do anything like that."

Aunt Grace shook her head. "My only hope is the detective's report will prove to Margaret once and for all how despicable the man is."

"My point exactly," Mr. Bradford said. "What is to prevent a man like that from breaking into this house this very minute, seizing Margaret, and running off with her?"

"What do you suggest?" Aunt Grace asked.

"It saddens me to say it," Mr. Bradford said. "But for her own good, I think Margaret should return to her room, and stay there in its safe confines, at least until she sees the error of her ways. Once Sebastian realizes he can't have his way with her, I'm sure he'll need little convincing to leave."

"No," Meg said. "Not back to my room. Can't I at least stay downstairs for the rest of today?"

"It's for your own good," Mr. Bradford declared.

Meg wanted to shout at him, to tell him to go away and leave her alone, but she knew the dangers if she made a scene. "Just for today," she whispered.

"It is to protect you," Aunt Grace said. "Both from Sebastian, and from your own baser instincts. Go upstairs at once, Margaret."

"I hate being locked in," Meg said.

"I know you think it's punishment," Aunt Grace said. "But it's not. Take your needlepoint with you. You can keep yourself just as busy there as down here."

Ordinarily, Meg was thrilled to be excused from Aunt Grace's company, but it felt so sweet to be with people again, even Grace, that she hated the thought of leaving. "May Clark come with me?" she asked.

"No," his father said. "Margaret, you must realize that while there's a cloud over your head, anybody associated with you suffers the same risk."

"You don't think Nicky is going to kidnap him?" Meg asked.

"I meant the loss of reputation," Mr. Bradford replied. "Really, Grace, what has gotten into the girl?"

"I'm sorry," Meg said. She got up and started to leave. Clark and his father both stood up, and Clark began walking out with her.

"I'm just seeing her to the stairs, Father," Clark said, and Meg knew what an act of courage those words were for Clark and felt grateful to him once again.

"Very well," Mr. Bradford said. "Youth is so impulsive," he declared to Aunt Grace as the teenagers left.

"And age is repulsive," Meg whispered, but Clark didn't laugh.

"You're in it this time," he said softly.

"Locked in it," Meg said.

Clark took her hand and passed a note to her. "Think about everything Father has said," he said in a normal voice. "Your aunt really does know what's best for you."

"Yes, Clark," Meg said. She tried desperately not to run up the stairs, to what had suddenly become the haven of her bedroom. Aunt Grace would be up momentarily, she knew, to check on her and lock the door. She had only moments to read the note, then find a place to hide it. But running would give away everything, so she paced her walk, not too fast, not too slow, and then left the door open behind her, the way Grace would want to find it.

Dearest Daisy,
It was a joy to see you, even in the rain. I love you, and will think about what you suggested.

Nicky

Meg clutched the note to her breast, then slipped it under her bed. Not even the sound of the key turning in the lock disturbed her. Nick would agree to marry her, and then there'd be no more prisons.

Chapter Nine

By Tuesday, Aunt Grace had decided Nick wasn't about to abduct Meg, and she eased her niece's restrictions. Meg was allowed out of her room during the day, and although she was locked in at night, and checked up on, she still reveled in her freedom. Playing the piano and walks in the garden were permitted again, and on Thursday, she was even allowed to go swimming. She was accompanied by two maids, and she wasn't allowed to wander off of Grace's private beachfront, but it didn't matter. She could move again, and she had Nick's note (cleverly hidden inside the toe of her right boot), to give her strength when she felt weakest.

Clark was still on the proscribed list (although Meg was of the opinion Mr. Bradford had made that rule up himself), and no other friends dropped by, but that was all right too. Meg couldn't imagine talking about anything other than Nick, and that was the one subject she knew was unwise to discuss. It was better to read and do needlepoint, take solitary walks and swims, than to destroy whatever chances she had left.

She yearned to be with Nick, but the risk was too great, and without Clark's cooperation, there was no way of making contact with him anyway. The day would come, Meg told herself again and again, the day would come when nothing Aunt Grace could think of would keep them apart. All Meg had to do was behave herself, so Grace's defenses would ease, and then she could make her escape. Mrs. Nick Sebastian. Just weeks away, maybe even days. Meg Sebastian. She and Nick together forever. She had fantasies all day long of their home together, the sacrifices they'd happily make for each other, the joys they'd share in each other's company. She had dreams at night of their lovemaking, not too explicit, since Meg was still a little hazy on the logistics of the act, but so full of heat and yearning that she'd wake up in her darkened room sweating with desire. Just weeks, she told herself. Maybe even days. And she held on to Nick's note.

Then on Friday, the amazing happened. There was a knock on the door, Delman opened it, and standing right there was Nick. Meg wanted to throw herself into his arms, his real, genuine, right-there arms, but Nick barely glanced at her, so Meg held herself back.

"Miss Winslow is expecting me," Nick said.

"Yes, sir," Delman replied. "Please come this way." He led Nick into Aunt Grace's sitting room, and Meg, not knowing what else to do, followed.

"Ah good, you're both here," Aunt Grace said. "Sit down, Mr. Sebastian. Can I offer you something to drink? Some iced tea perhaps?"

"No thank you," Nick said. "May I ask why you sent for me?"

"Certainly," Grace replied. "Margaret, sit by my side." So Meg did. The smell of Grace's powder overwhelmed her, but she knew better than to show weakness.

"As Margaret already knows, I have hired private investigators to check into your past," Grace said to Nick, as though this were the most ordinary of announcements. "I'm sure you understand how important it is for me to learn the background of any young man Margaret expresses an interest in."

"I'll take your word for it," Nick said. "It's not a habit my family ever got into."

"Ah yes," Grace said. "Your family. I must say they made for most interesting and colorful reading."

Nick smiled. "I'm glad they've proved good for something," he said. "But I still don't see why you asked me here. You have the report. Fling it around if you want, but it's no concern of mine. I certainly didn't sanction it."

"No, you certainly didn't," Grace said. "And that is why you were invited. I knew I could show it to Margaret, and she would find the vast discrepancies between the fairy tales you told us and the sordid realities the detectives uncovered. But she might not believe the report. Margaret has shown herself the past few days to be disrespectful, defiant, almost to the point of instability. Both my brother Marcus and I are quite concerned about her and her future, a future which, I can assure you, does not include you."

"I'm still waiting for your point," Nick said. Meg could hear the edge in his voice.

"I want you here while Margaret reads the report," Grace declared. "I have a copy for you as well, so if there are any inaccuracies, you can correct them. I don't want Margaret to think I in any way have attempted to deceive her. She will read the truth along with you, and I'm sure once she sees you for the money-hungry liar you are, she will never dream of you again."

"Aunt Grace," Meg said, but she had so many different things to protest, she couldn't finish the sentence.

"Margaret undoubtedly thinks of this as a public humiliation," Aunt Grace said to Nick. "She'll thank me for it one day. It is my obligation to save her from the likes of you."

"That's funny," Nick said. "I thought my obligation was to save her from the likes of you as well."

"I don't want to read the report," Meg said. "I'm sure everything in it is true. Please, Aunt Grace. Don't make me read it."

"It's for your own good," Aunt Grace replied. "You are still a very young girl, Margaret, and innocent in the ways of the world. Mr. Sebastian is merely the first of what may well prove to be a long line of men chasing you for your money. You stand to come into a substantial estate, unless I'm forced to disinherit you, in which case you will be nearly as penniless as Mr. Sebastian. Men of his ilk can smell money. They don't care whom they prey upon to satisfy their needs. Mr. Sebastian, coming as he does from an especially squalid background, has animal needs as well. I'm sorry you have to be exposed to such base human nature, but hard as I have tried to protect you, there is a wild streak to you, Margaret, no doubt encouraged by your parents, that forces me to take extra measures to save you from yourself. You know all I have done for you in the past, and you know all I am willing to do for you in the future. I suggest you read this report thoroughly. I shall observe your every response, and then discuss with Marcus what steps we should next take."

"I'm sorry," Meg said to Nick, grieving that he should have to see her in such a weakened position.

"It's all right," Nick replied. "The report should be amusing. My past is pretty much a farce."

"Your future undoubtedly will be one as well," Grace said. She walked over to her desk, picked up two copies of the report, and handed one each to Nick and Meg. Meg hated just touching it, but with Grace's eyes fixed on her, and knowing that one final glorious act of defiance could have her locked away for years, forced herself to begin to read.

> Nicholas George Sebastian was born George Nicholas Keefer on April 12, 1938. His mother was Mary Maud Keefer, aged twenty and two months at the time of his birth. His father was listed on the birth certificate as "unknown." However, his father was Sebastian Taylor Prescott, a well-to-do North Carolina businessman, whose secretary Miss Keefer had been. Miss Keefer accepted a payment of one thousand dollars, in exchange for which she did not list a father on her son's birth certificate.

Meg put the report down for a moment and willed herself not to give in to her nausea. It was bad enough seeing Nick's pathetic story there on paper, where Aunt Grace could gloat over it. But to have Nick in the same room, reading those same cruel words, was almost more than she could stand. She glanced over to him, and saw that he was skimming the report, looking for which awful detail she couldn't imagine, then reading the thing more thoroughly. If he felt pain or embarrassment, he wasn't showing it.

"Margaret," Aunt Grace said. "We don't have all day."

> Miss Keefer boarded her son out with various relatives while she moved from city to city. In 1946, she met and married former Pfc Harold Clay, of Wilmington, Delaware. She brought George home to live with her. In 1947, Mrs. Clay gave birth to a son, Harold, Jr. In 1949 she had a daughter, Diane.
>
> Mr. Clay worked at various factories in the Wilmington area. He drank heavily and was reputed to have a violent temper. George's school reports show he was a boy of unusual intelligence (his IQ was 148) but erratic temperament, occasionally doing brilliantly, frequently getting into trouble. It was believed family problems were at the root of George's behavior, and in 1950, after a social services investigation, George was put in foster care for six months until his mother sued to regain custody.

It was believed family problems were at the root, Meg thought, and her anger spread to include not only Grace and Marcus and Mr. Bradford, but those fools who looked at Nick's beautiful scarred face and didn't fight to save him. She hated not only his stepfather, Harold Clay, he had a name now, and his real father, Sebastian Taylor Prescott, who had a son and turned his back on him, but Nick's mother as well, and his teachers and the social workers, and everybody who didn't love Nick as she loved him. She wondered how many stories Nick had to tell, and how many he would ever be able to tell, even to her. She wondered how people could be so hateful.

> In January of 1954, Mary Keefer Clay died of cancer. While George Keefer's legal residence remained with his stepfather, in actuality he spent little time there, and on his sixteenth birthday, all connections were officially severed. Keefer lived in foster care until the end of that summer, and then moved on to be on his own. He lived in flophouses, stayed with friends, and when he had the funds, lived at the local YMCA. During this time, Keefer worked at a variety of part-time jobs, while continuing to attend high school. He maintained the fiction that he was still residing at Clay's address, and forged his stepfather's signature to report cards.

Nicky at sixteen, Meg thought. The age she was now. Meg knew she had suffered. The loss of her parents was something she felt every day, and suspected she would never completely get over. But everything else had been privilege. When her parents had died, there'd been no foster care, just genuinely concerned relatives. There was no disruption of her schooling. Even now, when she knew Marcus was disgusted with her, and Aunt Grace was at wits' end, there was never a suggestion that she was no longer a family member. No flophouses for Margaret Louise Winslow. Just no love, no understanding. Well, hell, who needed love and understanding. See how far Nick had come without any.

A complete list of Keefer's places of employment can be found at the end of this report (Document D). Among other jobs, he washed dishes, worked as a busboy, caddied at the local country club, and delivered groceries.

No wonder they thought Isabelle would be attracted to him, Meg thought, then blushed at her disloyalty.

Keefer's work was regarded as satisfactory, and he left each job of his own volition. The general impression he gave was that he was "too good" for that kind of labor and that his ambitions were great. He had few friends, although it was agreed that he could be quite charming when he so chose.

What are his ambitions, Meg wondered. What was it Nick wanted, other than her and Princeton. There was so much they still had to learn about each other. Whatever those ambitions were, Meg intended to be a full partner in them.

Keefer graduated seventh in his class (his ranking at the end of junior year had been second). He had been admitted to Princeton, but had not requested scholarship aid.

After graduating from high school, Keefer disappeared from sight for a month or so. He was next reported visiting the office of Sebastian Prescott. According to Audrey Williams, Mr. Prescott's secretary, on August 3, 1955, George Keefer came to Mr. Prescott's office, demanding an interview with him. Miss Williams said the resemblance between the two men was startling, and assuming that they must be related, she sent Keefer in. She was able to overhear much of their conversation. Keefer threatened to reveal his identity to Prescott's wife, son, and daughter, unless Prescott paid for his education at Princeton.

Meg put the report down again. She knew she was in virgin territory, that Nick had intended to tell her all this, but Clark had interrupted him, and they hadn't discussed it since. She didn't think Nick had mentioned this other set of a half brother and a half sister. How Nick must have hated them all, those four children who had fathers they could call their own. She knew something then that Nick himself might not have known, how important it was for him to have a family, and she vowed she would give him children who would love Nick as she did. More than anybody she knew, he was entitled.

Miss Williams informed us that Mr. Prescott was at that time suffering from marital problems.

Serves him right, Meg thought.

Apparently he felt that Keefer's arrival in his family life was inopportune. However, he refused to give Keefer the full four-years' tuition, instead making out a check for three thousand dollars, telling Keefer that that was all he'd ever see from him, and that if he knew what was good for him, he'd take the money, change his name, leave town, and never bother decent people again. Miss Williams informed us that she had never heard Mr. Prescott so angry. Disillusioned by the way he had treated his own, albeit illegitimate son, Miss Williams left Prescott's employ shortly thereafter.

We have been unable to find any records of George Keefer or Nicholas Sebastian for the next twelve months. In September of 1956, however, he registered at Princeton University as a freshman, under the name of Nicholas George Sebastian. He listed himself as an orphan, and paid the full year's tuition himself, claiming he had received the funds from a trust fund set up for him by his former English teacher, Mr. John Wilson. There were no John Wilsons in the Wilmington school district that Keefer attended, so presumably he invented the entire story. Mr. Sebastian has not worked any part-time jobs since he began at Princeton, and his tuition is completely paid for the upcoming academic year, so he must have been able to increase the amount of his savings from that initial three thousand dollars. We are trying to determine if illegal activities were involved, but thus far have been unable to uncover any.

Meg realized then that that was what Nick had skimmed through trying to find. There was a year of his life he hadn't told her about, a year he didn't want her to know of. Meg knew there was nothing Nick could reveal that would make her love him any the less, but the existence of that year frightened her. It was ironic that all the horrible facts about Nick's parents and past had no power to scare her, but that the unknown year was Aunt Grace's strongest weapon. Meg hoped she could keep Grace from finding that out.

> Mr. Sebastian is popular with his classmates at Princeton, and academically is doing quite well, with a 3.6 average. His friends there are of the impression that he comes from an impoverished but socially prominent family in the Midwest, that his father died on D-day, and his mother, his junior year in high school.

I have no friends, he'd told her, and that was not a lie. How can you call someone a friend who doesn't know anything honest about you.

> His lack of family does not seem to be held against him, and the feeling is he'll do well in whatever field he chooses to make his own.

Meg realized she was crying. She slammed the report down, and prayed Nick wouldn't misunderstand her tears. Since she wasn't sure what the tears signified, she could only hope he knew her better than she knew herself.

"I see you've finished," Aunt Grace said. "I assume from the time you took, you read the report quite thoroughly."

Meg nodded. Aunt Grace handed her a handkerchief. It smelled of her powder.

"The story you told us was quite different," Aunt Grace said. "Can you account for those discrepancies, Mr. Sebastian?"

Nick smiled. "I lied," he said.

"Then you do not dispute the detective's report?" she asked.

"It's substantially accurate," he said. "But I graduated fourth in my class, not seventh." He paused for a moment. "That's important to me," he said. "It wasn't easy, getting my schoolwork done that year."

"Fourth," Aunt Grace said. "I shall inform the detective agency of their error. Are there any others?"

"No," Nick said. "It's all there."

"I hope you're satisfied, Margaret," Aunt Grace said. "This young man, who presented himself as a paragon of virtue, from the finest families of the South and Midwest, is nothing more than the cheap by-product of a tawdry affair. Decent people come from decent families. It's as simple as that."

Meg knew it wasn't simple at all. She wiped the tears off her cheeks and hoped Nick had some understanding of how much she loved him, how unshakable that love was.

"Well, Margaret," Aunt Grace said. "I'm sure Mr. Sebastian is as eager as I am to learn your reaction to this report."

Meg wanted to tell Grace that she knew already all those miserable facts, that the one gift Nick had given her was honesty. She was about to say it when Nick shook his head almost imperceptibly, and Meg realized that Grace had made a fatal error forcing Nick to be there with her. Without Nick, Meg would have allowed her fury to control her, and Grace would have decided she was unstable (most ghastly of euphemisms). And in a way, Grace would have been right, because what Meg wanted to do was physically assault Grace, batter her, kill her if she could. The depth of her anger frightened Meg. There were so many emotions inside her she'd forbidden herself from feeling, and because of Nick, thanks to Nick, she could feel them all, the bad ones as well as the good. But Nick was there to protect her. Because of his love, Meg would never hurt Grace, would never hurt herself again. Because of Nick, Meg could feel and still survive.

"It's very upsetting," Meg finally said. "You knew it would be."

"I know nothing about you anymore," Aunt Grace replied. "Your actions have been a mystery to me for days now."

Meg nodded. "I'm sorry," she said. Would her life ever cease being an apology? "I know I've caused you a great deal of worry. I . . . I believed in him, in everything he told me." She hoped Grace wouldn't push too hard, not wanting to have to lie, especially in front of Nick.

"So you see now what sort of man he is," Aunt Grace said.

"Yes," Meg said. "I see."

"And you admit I have been correct in my fears," Aunt Grace continued. "That I can tell what sort of man is proper for you, and what sort most emphatically is not."

"Your fears were right," Meg said, and she began to cry again.

"Very well," Aunt Grace said. "This is not a happy moment for me either, Margaret. I hope we shall never have to reenact this scene. A lesson so bitterly learned should be remembered for the rest of your life."

"I'll never forget it," Meg choked out. She was sobbing now, for her own anguish, and for Nick's.

"There is no need for you to carry on so," Aunt Grace said. "Especially in front of a stranger. Margaret, go to your room. I'll be up momentarily, to discuss what we have both found out, and what punishments we deem appropriate for your recent misbehavior."

"Stop it," Nick said. "Can't you see you've hurt her enough?"

"This is none of your concern," Aunt Grace declared. "Margaret, go to your room. Mr. Sebastian and I are about to discuss what fee he will accept to leave Eastgate and forget this whole wretched business."

"Aunt Grace!" Meg cried, but Nick only laughed.

"No fee is necessary, Miss Winslow," he said, getting up from the chair, and returning his copy of the report to her. "Thank you anyway." He didn't even look at Meg as he walked away.

CHAPTER TEN

Sleep was impossible that night. Meg paced her locked room over and over, trying to avoid thinking about the detective's report that Aunt Grace had cunningly returned to her at lunchtime. Not that Meg had seen her then, or anytime until 10:30 lights-out. Meg had stayed in her room all day, and Grace was apparently disturbed enough by the sounds of her sobs to avoid her. It was the one thing Meg had for comfort. She didn't know what she would have done if Grace had decided to discuss Nick's sordid past or her own miserable future just then.

Grace did come in for a few minutes at 10:30, though. "Have you reread the report?" she asked.

"Yes," Meg said, wishing it were a lie.

Grace glanced at the tearstained, crumpled report, and was satisfied Meg had indeed read it. "Life is difficult," she declared. "The poor are always going on about unjust conditions, but suffering knows no social class."

Meg stared at Grace.

"I know the pain you're feeling," Grace said. "I too was young once. I too had suitors."

"Like Nick?" Meg asked.

"There was a man my parents deemed unacceptable," Aunt Grace said. "His parents came from a fine family, don't misunderstand me, but they were divorced, and his mother had married an Italian. A count, I believe, but it didn't matter. My parents were not about to allow their only daughter to marry a man whose parents were divorced. Let alone with an Italian stepfather."

"Did you love him?" Meg asked. Aunt Grace never spoke about her youth except to lecture Meg. As far as Meg knew, Grace had grown up obeying her elders, never mumbling or stooping, and doing all that was required of her. No love, no rebellion, no imperfections.

Aunt Grace looked thoughtful. "I don't know," she said. "At the time, I was sure I did. There were nights I cried in this very room. But I knew my parents were correct."

"Why?" Meg asked. "He hadn't done anything wrong. It wasn't his fault his parents were divorced."

"Breeding is everything," Aunt Grace replied. "A man whose mother marries an Italian is far more likely to stray from convention than one whose mother does not." She paused for a moment. "My parents were very conservative," she declared. "Within just a few years, it seemed everybody was getting divorced and marrying Italians, and society no longer seemed to stand for anything. Had I been Reggie's age, or even Marcus's, I could have married anybody I chose."

"But times are different now," Meg said. "Standards are different."

Aunt Grace took Meg's hand and held it for a moment in what came as close to tenderness as the two of them could achieve. "He's illegitimate," Grace said. "I'm sure you know the gutter word for that. I spoke to the head of the detective agency. He told me things that weren't put in the report, about his mother. She took money from men in exchange for . . . the marriage act. It is no surprise that his father turned his back on the girl and her child. I'm not saying I condone his behavior. I'm sure different arrangements could have been made. But a boy with a mother like that, a boy with no father, cannot possibly have a moral code. Do you think his stepfather taught him the difference between right and wrong?"

Meg shook her head

"I want you to be happy," Grace said. "I know you don't believe that, but it's true. You could never be happy with a man like that. You are a Winslow. We stand for something. He is a man without family, without even a name. There will be other boys, Margaret."

"There weren't for you," Meg said, knowing it was a hurtful remark, and regretting it almost as soon as she said it.

Grace rose and looked down at her niece. "Tomorrow is Saturday," she declared. "We will discuss then the best way to teach you respect for your elders."

"Aunt Grace, I'm sorry," Meg said.

"You have a great deal to be sorry for," Aunt Grace replied. "And there is much you have yet to learn. You may keep your light on an extra half hour this evening to give you the chance to reread the report one more time. Perhaps once you realize the sort of man I have saved you from, you will cease being hostile, and begin to feel gratitude instead."

"Yes, Aunt Grace," Meg said with a sigh.

Aunt Grace walked to the door, but before opening it, turned to face Meg one more time. "He is a wicked man," she said. "He has been corrupted, and wishes only to corrupt. You are most fortunate to have family to protect you. Good night, Margaret."

"Good night, Aunt Grace," Meg said. She listened to the key being turned, then, as she was instructed, reread the report. She wondered if Nick knew what his mother had done, wondered what burst of kindness had kept the agency from writing it up. In spite of herself, she wondered about the year Nick had chosen not to tell her about. In spite of herself, she wondered how she could ever survive without him.

She turned her light off at eleven, but she was too restless, too frightened, to even try to sleep. She walked around her room instead, until shortly after midnight, when she heard noises outside her bedroom window.

She ran to the window and looked down. There was Nick struggling to put a ladder in place.

Meg bit down on her lip to keep from laughing. She went to her closet and slipped a blouse and skirt on, then located her sneakers and put them on as well. She unlatched the window, and once Nick gestured that it was safe, climbed down the ladder.

Nick grabbed for her on the bottom two rungs, and they held each other tightly for as long as they dared. Then they hid the ladder, and ran away from the house, toward the beach. They didn't speak until they were past the point where anybody in Aunt Grace's house could see or hear them.

"I was so afraid," Nick said as they huddled together

by the ocean. "I thought that after you read the report, you'd never want to see me again."

"All I wanted was to see you," Meg said. "To see you, to talk to you, to love you."

"You don't hate me, then?" Nick asked.

"How could I?" Meg asked. "How could I hate you when I love you so much? And besides, you told me everything there was in that report." Well, almost everything, she thought.

"It looked different seeing it like that," Nick said. "Hell, I lived through it, and it still looked different. Uglier." He laughed his harsh, humorless laugh. "I pride myself on keeping clean," he said. "I know that doesn't seem like a big deal to you, but it always has been to me. My stepfather stank from sweat and whiskey and just plain meanness, and sometimes bills didn't get paid and the hot water was turned off, but I always stayed clean. No matter where I lived, no matter how I lived, I stayed clean. This morning, reading that report, I felt dirty, slimy. I could smell the gutter in me."

Meg stroked his hair. "I smelled Aunt Grace," she said. "The scent of her powder nauseated me."

Nick smiled. "Maybe that was it," he said. "Maybe that was what I sensed."

"I tried to show you how much I love you," Meg declared. "I was so afraid you'd see me crying and not understand why."

"I don't understand anything anymore," Nick said. "I used to know just who I was and where I was going, but now all that counts is you. I'd give up everything for you, Daisy. I know that doesn't sound like much. I don't have family or friends or money or any of those things most people have to give up. But I have my dreams, and I'd give them up for you."

"You don't have to," Meg said. "Your dreams are mine. I want only what you want."

They kissed hungrily. "Love me," she whispered. "I want to make love with you."

But Nick broke away. "I want that too," he said. "You wouldn't believe how much I want that. But not now. Not like this."

"Why not?" Meg demanded.

"For a lot of reasons," Nick said. "All of which I've thought about for days now. What if you got pregnant? What if I got arrested? What if your aunt and that wonderful uncle Marcus of yours found out and used that as proof of your mental instability? What if once we started we couldn't stop?"

"Then it has nothing to do with my purity?" Meg asked.

Nick grinned. "That purity of yours is just an inconvenience," he said. "We'll take care of it at the right moment."

Meg cuddled up beside him. "I don't want to wait too long," she said. "I don't think I could stand waiting too long."

"Me neither," Nick replied. He bent over, and kissed Meg lightly on her lips. "We'll be together," he said. "I promise."

"I promise too," Meg said. She stared out at the ocean. "Aunt Grace was almost human tonight," she said. "Just for a moment or two. She talked about a boy she had loved and how her parents wouldn't let them get married because his parents were divorced and his mother married an Italian."

"An organ-grinder?" Nick asked.

"A count," Meg replied. "My grandparents had very high standards."

"So it would seem," Nick said. "At least we don't have them to deal with."

"She almost didn't scare me when we talked like that," Meg said. "I hate how scared I am of Aunt Grace. Sometimes when we're together, you and me and her, I don't feel frightened anymore, but that's because you're there. As soon as you're gone, I'm scared again."

Nick nodded. "She is scary," he said. "She has so much power over you. She scares me, what she could do to you, how she could hurt you. How she has hurt you already."

"Aunt Grace hasn't hurt me," Meg replied. "Not the way your stepfather hurt you."

"Oh Daisy," Nick said. "There are so many different ways of hurting. Not all wounds come from iron skillets. You have no idea how wonderful you are. I'm glad, in a way, because if you did, you wouldn't have fallen in love with me. But that's Grace's fault. That's how she's hurt you. She's made you feel inadequate, frightened. Someday you'll realize just what she's done to you, and you'll hate her almost as much as I do."

"I hate your stepfather," Meg said. "Even more than you do, I think. And I hate your father, too, and I hate your mother for letting all those things happen to you."

"You shouldn't hate my mother," Nick said. "I don't. She told me when she was dying that she was sorry she didn't love me, but I think she did. I think she must have, to feel regrets like that. And she used to hug me when I was little. I didn't see that much of her, but when I did, when she'd come to see me, she almost always hugged me. So don't hate her, all right?"

"All right," Meg said. She thought of the conversation she'd had with Aunt Grace, and in spite of herself, she asked, "Nicky, who taught you the difference between right and wrong?"

"You did," Nick replied.

Meg nodded. That was what Aunt Grace couldn't understand, how much Nick had already taught her, and how much she had in turn taught Nick. "We have to make a plan," she said. "We have to work out our future. Aunt Grace says tomorrow we're going to decide how to teach me to respect my elders. She brought up gratitude again."

"Has she been keeping you locked up?" Nick asked. "I saw Clark yesterday, and he said he thought things were easing up."

"They have been," Meg said. "A lot depends on the next few days. But even if I behave myself, I'm still going to be sent to England in August, and I may not get back to the States for two years."

"Better that than the sanitarium," Nick said.

"You sound like Aunt Grace," Meg said. "The lesser of two evils is still evil, Nicky."

"You still want to get married?" Nick asked.

"Please," Meg said. "We could run off tonight, and they'd never find us."

"Not tonight," Nick replied. "We're taking too big a risk just being here together. They're bound to check up on you tonight."

"Tomorrow night, then," Meg said. "Soon, Nicky. It's our only chance."

"Daytime is better than night," Nick said. "If you

behave yourself tomorrow, act penitent, then your aunt will be sure to let you go to church on Sunday."

"I'll never be able to escape on Sunday," Meg said. "Aunt Grace will practically chain me to her all day."

"And you'll keep on behaving yourself," Nick said. "You'll show her how much the report upset you, how you've realized what I'm really like. You've started that already, haven't you? You haven't been leaping to my defense, or anything."

"I don't think so," Meg said. "I've been too scared to do much of anything today. I was so afraid I'd never see you again."

"Don't ever be scared of that," Nick said. "I don't know how we're going to arrange things, Daisy. I don't know how it's all going to work out. But one way or another, we'll be together. I'm going to marry you, and I'm never going to spend a night apart from you. I need you too much. Without you, I'm nothing."

"I know," Meg said. "I'm nothing without you. That's what frightens me so."

Nick kissed her. "You're everything," he said. "You're strong and brave and beautiful. If you ever feel frightened or alone, tell yourself that, that you're strong and brave and beautiful. Will you do that for me?"

"I'm strong and brave and beautiful," Meg said. It sounded better coming from Nick. "I wish there were words I could teach you. But you already know you're smart and handsome and loving."

"No," Nick said. "I didn't know I was loving."

"Now you know," Meg said, and she laughed with triumph. She had given Nick something of value, something no one could ever take away from him. She still owed him so much, but at least part of the debt had been paid off. "So Sunday I'm penitent. Does that mean we can get married on Monday?"

"We'd better aim for Tuesday instead," Nick said. "We'll need Clark's cooperation. I hate to rely on him, but he seems to be the only friend you have that Grace will trust you with."

"Clark isn't going to like it," Meg said.

"I know," Nick replied. "But he loves you, and I think you can count on him. Besides, without him, we don't have a chance. You'll see Clark on Sunday at church. Make a date with him for Tuesday. Talk to Grace about it first, get clearance from her, and if she says yes, then ask Clark."

"What if she says no?" Meg asked.

"We still have four weeks before you'll leave for England," Nick said. "We don't have to rush things."

"Yes we do," Meg declared. "If I don't get out of that house soon, I probably will go mad." She realized uncomfortably that she wasn't joking, and wondered if Nicky understood that as well.

"It will work out," he said. "We'll try for Tuesday."

Meg thought for a moment. "No, Thursday," she said. "Thursday will be better. The staff has Thursdays off, so there are fewer people to check up on me. And it gives me more time to convince Aunt Grace."

"Can you manage until Thursday?" Nick asked.

Meg nodded. "If I know we're really getting married then, I can," she said. "Promise me, Nicky. Promise me we're getting married."

"Thursday," he said. "By Friday you'll be Mrs. Nick Sebastian. By Friday we'll be together for the rest of our lives."

"Then I can hold out until Thursday," Meg said. "All

right. Thursday morning, I go out with Clark. We'll tell Grace we're going to have lunch together, and she shouldn't expect us back until supper. That should work out well. Aunt Grace always lunches out on Thursdays, and then we have a light supper, so it makes sense that Clark and I would stay out as well. Only as soon as Clark and I leave, we'll meet you, and you and I will leave Eastgate. Maybe I can take some money with me. Aunt Grace usually has some money lying around in her bedroom. She likes to leave it there as temptation for the servants."

"No money," Nick said. "Just whatever's in your pocketbook. Things are risky enough without theft charges."

"Then how will we manage?" Meg asked. "We'll need transportation to wherever we're going."

"I have the money for that," Nick replied.

"If you have money, then why are you staying in a boardinghouse?" Meg asked.

"I have enough money to get me through Princeton," Nick said. "Enough for clothes and food as long as I'm careful. Nobody expects me to be rich there, but I can't seem like a bum either. But if I'm not going back to Princeton, then I certainly have the funds to pay for bus tickets for both of us, and a couple of nights at a hotel somewhere as our honeymoon, and then an apartment for us until I can get a job."

"I'll get the job," Meg said. "You have to complete your education."

"I'm not spending the rest of my life with a high-school dropout," Nick said. "I'll work, you'll finish school. I can take night classes somewhere. Don't worry. We'll both end up with as many degrees as we want."

"So we take a bus," Meg said. She'd argue with Nick

about his education some other time. "And we get married, and then we disappear. I don't care where we live, just as long as we're together."

"Neither do I," Nick said. "Maybe we'll stick a pin in a map and find our home that way."

"Home," Meg said.

Nick smiled. "I know," he said. "It is an amazing word."

"I'll make you a beautiful home," Meg promised him. "I'll make you a home you'll always be happy in."

"You have to get back," Nick said. "If Grace finds out you're gone, we'll both be in big trouble."

"I know," Meg said. "I love you so much, Nicky."

"I love you, Daisy," he said. "Mrs. Nick Sebastian. Now let's get you to your room."

"Kiss me first," she said, and he did.

"Mrs. Nick Sebastian," Meg whispered to herself as she and Nick hugged for one last time. "Mrs. Nick Sebastian." Those three words held a universe of promise for her, a universe she'd enter into in less than a week.

CHAPTER ELEVEN

Meg awoke the next morning to find her bedroom door unlocked. After showering off any remaining sand from the night before, and dressing, she went downstairs and had breakfast with Aunt Grace.

"How did you sleep?" Grace asked as she finished her second cup of coffee. It was a more personal question than Meg was accustomed to.

"Not very well," Meg replied. "I had a lot to think about."

"And did you reach any conclusions?" Aunt Grace asked.

Meg thought of all the conclusions she had reached and tried not to smile. "I hope I didn't disturb you," she said. "I woke up a couple of times and reread the report. I'm sorry I turned the light back on."

"It's understandable given the circumstances," Aunt Grace said. "I'm sure you won't make a habit of it.

Keeping late hours is most unhealthy for a girl your age."

Meg nodded. "I felt compelled to read it again and again," she said.

"Ordinarily, one should not give in to compulsion," Aunt Grace declared. "But these were unusual circumstances. Did you feel the need to read it again this morning?"

Did everything have to be a land mine with Aunt Grace? "Not this morning," Meg said. "Not after three A.M., really. It was then that I realized just how much I owed you, how kind and generous you've been to me."

"And what led you to that conclusion?" Aunt Grace asked.

Bald-faced lying, Meg wanted to reply. Even the truth, that she did feel a touch of gratitude when she compared her childhood to Nick's, wouldn't do as an answer. "I really thought I loved him," she said, not even willing to mention Nick's name to Grace. "And thanks to you and your willingness to hire those detectives, I discovered that all I loved was a pack of lies."

Aunt Grace nodded. She clearly expected more.

"I'm very young," Meg said, choosing her words carefully, aiming for that level of groveling that Aunt Grace would find most appealing. "I think sometimes that I know what's best for me, but that's just foolishness. Foolishness I hope I'll outgrow, especially with your guidance. Without an aunt, without a guardian, like you, protecting me, teaching me, I might make all kinds of reckless mistakes. The reckless mistakes of youth."

"Yes?" Aunt Grace said. She appeared insatiable.

"And I suppose I've inherited my parents' reckless natures as well," Meg said. She hated Aunt Grace then with a clarity that startled even her. "What I always thought of as being adventuresome was really being irresponsible." She offered a thousand silent apologies to the memory of her beautiful, perfect parents.

"You've given this matter a great deal of thought," Aunt Grace said. "And I am impressed with how well you worded those thoughts. None of the mumbling I've gotten accustomed to from you. I'm pleased to see this new spirit in you, Margaret. It bodes well for your future."

"Thank you, Aunt Grace," Meg said.

"Very well," Aunt Grace said. "From now on, there will be no need for us to discuss Mr. Sebastian again. I don't doubt that there will be moments you'll think of him, romance is like that, but your life is on its proper course once again, and you will not stray from it."

"No, Aunt Grace," Meg said.

"However, you still have many acts you must atone for," Aunt Grace stated. "Come with me to the morning room, and we'll discuss there what must be done next."

Meg left her half-finished breakfast and followed her aunt into the room where less than twenty-four hours before they'd all sat around reading the detective's report. Aunt Grace sat on her customary chair, and indicated to Meg that she should sit on the same chair Nick had used. It comforted Meg to remember him there.

Aunt Grace closed the door, which meant that she didn't care for the servants overhearing. Meg marveled that Grace could think there were still some secrets worth preserving after the past few days.

"Your remorse appears genuine," Aunt Grace said. "Of course it might simply be inspired by fear of your future."

"I am afraid," Meg replied. She was, too, although the

idea of Thursday was keeping her strong enough to be dishonest.

"I spoke to Marcus yesterday," Aunt Grace said. "Naturally he wanted to know what your response was to the report. I intend to speak to him today as well, and inform him of our conversation."

Meg nodded.

"I was concerned about your crying," Aunt Grace declared. "I thought you had succumbed to hysteria, and might be better off in a more peaceful surrounding. But Marcus said that his wife and daughters frequently wept over the most trivial matters, and unless you continued to cry, it was probably not a sign of constitutional weakness."

"I'm sorry if I worried you, Aunt Grace," Meg said. Had she been that close to the sanitarium and not even realized it?

"You're mumbling again, Margaret," Aunt Grace said. "No wonder your appeal is only to men of the lower classes. You must learn to speak clearly if you wish any sort of social success."

Meg felt herself shriveling inside. I am strong and brave and beautiful, she told herself, but without Nick in the room, she didn't believe it.

"Marcus and I remain uncertain what the nature of your punishment should be," Aunt Grace told Meg. "Marcus has a very kind heart, you know, and he feels that if you have indeed learned your lesson, there is no need for undue harshness on our parts."

Meg nodded. She didn't dare cry again, but it was hard to look at Aunt Grace and not start weeping.

"Raise your head, Margaret," Aunt Grace said. "I expect you to look at me while I'm speaking to you."

"Yes, Aunt Grace," Meg replied. Nicky loves me, she told herself. On Thursday we'll be married.

"I have two tasks for you this morning," Aunt Grace declared. "How you perform them will go a long way in determining what the next few weeks will be like."

"Yes, Aunt Grace," Meg said.

"They are both in the forms of apologies," Aunt Grace said. "First, you are to write a letter of remorse and appreciation to Marcus. It is the very least that you owe him. You will write it here, and I'll read it as soon as you are finished."

Meg nodded. "That's a good idea," she said. "Thank you."

"Then we are expected at the Bradford cottage," Aunt Grace said. "Where you will apologize to Mr. Bradford for the rude manner with which you addressed him last Sunday."

In Meg's memory, Mr. Bradford was the rude one, bursting into her house to repeat nasty gossip, but she knew better than to protest. "You're right," she said instead. "I owe him an apology. Thank you again."

"Very well," Aunt Grace said. "There is stationery and a pen waiting for you. Make your note short to Marcus. He is a busy man and has better things to do with his time than to read letters from foolish girls."

Then why are you making me write one? Meg thought, but she walked over to Aunt Grace's desk, picked up the pen, and carefully worded her note.

July 12

Dear Uncle Marcus,

For the past two weeks, I have been a burden upon both Aunt Grace and you, and I want to apologize for my rebellious and unthinking behavior.

"Be certain to denounce Mr. Sebastian in your note," Aunt Grace said. "Marcus will want to see that you've come to your senses."

"Yes, Aunt Grace," Meg replied.

I had the misfortune to meet a young man at my birthday party who, because of his charm and good looks, made me forget who I am and what my obligations are.

I cannot denounce you, Nicky, she thought, not the way Aunt Grace wants me to.

Because of the firm, yet loving, guidance that you and Aunt Grace have given me throughout your years of guardianship, I was able to see the error of my ways.

I know my behavior of late has been inexcusable, and I can never make up for the worry and alarm I have caused you. But I shall try everything in my powers to erase this shameful experience from your memory.

The love and kindness you have shown me since my parents' deaths have been a constant beacon of strength for me. I know how fortunate I am to have you as my uncle.

With much love and gratitude,

Margaret

She handed the note to Aunt Grace, who read it quickly. "I see you mention Mr. Sebastian's good looks and charm," she said. "But you seem to have left out his squalid background and deceit."

"I'm sorry," Meg said.

"Marcus will not believe you're sincere unless you show him you understand Mr. Sebastian's true nature," Aunt Grace said. "And frankly, neither will I."

The only way they'll believe me is if I lie, Meg thought. She took a second sheet of paper and wrote a new paragraph on it.

Because of the loving vigilance that you and Aunt Grace have shown, I was able to learn of the young man's lack of breeding and dishonest nature. His like will never deceive me again.

Aunt Grace read the paragraph. "That's better," she said. "But Marcus will expect you to mention how he was merely after your money."

"Why?" Meg protested.

"You are not in a position to demand explanations," Aunt Grace replied. "However, I'll give you one. Marcus is an extremely wealthy man, far richer than I, and he has the rich man's worry that his children will all wed gold diggers. His most recurring complaint to me over the past few days has been that with his own children to worry about, now you were forcing him to worry about you as well. If you tell him you understand that Mr. Sebastian was interested merely in your fortune, should I choose to leave my estate to you, Marcus will feel a great sense of relief. So for his sake, as well as your own, rewrite the paragraph."

"Yes, Aunt Grace," Meg said.

> Because of the loving vigilance that you and Aunt Grace have shown, I was able to learn of the young man's lack of breeding and dishonest nature. Painful though this is for me to admit, he was obviously after my money and had no real feelings for me. His like will never deceive me again.

"Excellent," Aunt Grace said. "Now write out three copies, one for Marcus, one for me, and one for yourself. You need only address one envelope."

"Yes, Aunt Grace," Meg said.

"And be sure to use your best penmanship," Aunt Grace said. "You're very careless crossing your t's, Margaret."

"Thank you, Aunt Grace," Meg said. She wrote the three copies, signed them all, then handed them to Aunt Grace for inspection. Grace nodded, took one for herself, and gave Meg an envelope, which she then addressed.

"I shall not be able to prompt you when you apologize to Mr. Bradford," Aunt Grace said. "Perhaps it might be wise if we rehearsed your remarks here, so that you will say the appropriate things to him."

"I'm to apologize for my rudeness," Meg said. "Is there anything else I need to say?"

"Mr. Bradford was kind enough to warn you of Mr. Sebastian's true nature," Aunt Grace said. "Don't you think you should thank him for that?"

"I'm sorry, Aunt Grace," Meg said. "Of course I should."

"Very well," she said. "Say to me what you will say to Mr. Bradford."

Meg nodded. "I'm sorry, Mr. Bradford," she began.

"Stand up, Margaret," Aunt Grace said.

"I'm sorry," Meg said, standing up by the desk. "I mean, I'm sorry, Mr. Bradford."

"Look at me when you speak," Aunt Grace said. "I do not understand why you find the floor so endlessly fascinating."

"Yes, Aunt Grace," Meg said. She forced herself to look up. "I'm sorry, Mr. Bradford, for my rude behavior last Sunday."

"Don't lick your lips," Aunt Grace said. "A disgusting habit."

"I'm sorry," Meg said. "I didn't realize."

"There's a great deal you fail to realize," Aunt Grace declared. "William Bradford is a very important man in Boston. Had it not been for his childhood friendship with Reggie, I doubt he would have allowed any closeness between you and Clark. That closeness could someday result in marriage, a match which might ordinarily be beyond your expectations. No matter how fine your family is, Margaret, you are penniless and dependent on the charity of others."

"I'm very grateful," Meg said.

"William Bradford will expect you to show him some

of that gratitude as well," Aunt Grace said. "He did not have to come here on Sunday to warn us of Mr. Sebastian's misdeeds. He could simply have forbidden Clark to have any future contact with you, which he may still do, unless you can convince him that you are genuinely apologetic for your behavior on Sunday, and that you realize it is only his kindness that allows you your friendship with Clark."

"Yes, Aunt Grace," Meg said.

"You might also think about that friendship with Clark," Grace declared. "And how it and it alone may save your place in society. For if the Bradfords turn their backs to you, then you can be sure you will never be welcome in the better homes again."

On Thursday, I'm marrying Nicky, Meg thought, but the longer she stayed talking with Aunt Grace, the harder it was to believe in that dream.

"Now say to me what you will say to William Bradford," Aunt Grace said. "Without mumbling, Margaret, or staring down at the floor."

Meg took a moment to compose herself. "I wish to apologize for my rudeness on Sunday, Mr. Bradford," she said. "I know how kind it was of you to come to my aunt's house and warn us about Mr. Sebastian." She glanced at Aunt Grace to see if that was enough.

"Go on," Aunt Grace said. "You have far more than that to be grateful for."

"I've always appreciated the generosity you and Mrs. Bradford have shown me over the years," Meg said. "Allowing me into your home, treating me almost as a member of your family."

"That's good," Aunt Grace said. "Now mention how

wrong it was of you to reject such kindness with your thoughtless words on Sunday."

"It was wrong of me to reject such kindness with my thoughtless words on Sunday," Meg said.

"William will want to hear that he was right about Mr. Sebastian," Aunt Grace declared.

"Does he know about the detective's report?" Meg asked.

"He knows I arranged for an investigation," Aunt Grace replied. "He thought it was an excellent idea. I haven't felt the need to tell him what the report actually said, but you should acknowledge that you've learned Mr. Sebastian's true nature, and that Mr. Bradford was right all the time."

Meg sighed.

"And don't merely parrot my words," Aunt Grace said. "I do not find that amusing."

"Yesterday, I had the opportunity to learn the truth about Mr. Sebastian's past," Meg said. Don't cry, she told herself. Don't cry or mumble or lick your lips or stare at the floor. "I learned that he'd lied to me and to Aunt Grace about who he was, and where he'd come from."

"Be specific, Margaret," Aunt Grace said. "William will undoubtedly be curious."

"Aunt Grace, please," Meg said.

"You do not seem to understand you are in no position to negotiate," Aunt Grace declared. "These apologies are tests, Margaret, tests you must pass if you wish to return to any semblance of your previous life. If you fail these tests, then I will be forced to admit I can no longer handle you, and you will be sent away to a place where there are professionals trained to handle the emotionally disturbed. They remain on call, Margaret. You could be there by dinnertime tonight."

"I'm sorry, Aunt Grace," Meg said. "What do you want me to say to Mr. Bradford? I'll say it, I swear I will."

"I think perhaps we should go there right now," Aunt Grace replied. "William Bradford is not the only one who needs convincing right now of your sincerity." She rang for the chauffeur, and in moments, she and Meg were being driven the short distance to the Bradford cottage.

The Bradford butler let them in, and Meg found herself standing in front of Mr. and Mrs. Bradford, and Clark, in their parlor.

"Thank you very much for seeing me," Meg began. "I hope I haven't disrupted your plans in any way." It scared her to look at Mr. Bradford, so she glanced at Mrs. Bradford instead, and noticed, not for the first time, how watery her eyes were. She wanted to look at Clark, but didn't dare, so she turned to face his father instead.

"We're very interested to hear what you have to say, Margaret," Mr. Bradford declared.

"Thank you," Meg said. "I appreciate that. I know I've been a worry to you, to all the people who are kind enough to care about me. I know I don't always show how grateful I am to you, for the way you've welcomed me into your home on so many occasions. Your friendship means so much to me. My father . . . well, I know how much he cherished that friendship, and how grateful he'd be to you for all you've done for me."

"Reggie was a good man," Mr. Bradford said. "A bit wild, perhaps, and I never did care for that wife of his, but a good man. Breeding does show."

Meg nodded. "That's one of the things I've been learning," she said. "About the importance of breeding, of where you come from and how it makes you what you are. I guess I've always taken it for granted. I guess that's why I couldn't see through Nick Sebastian as easily as you could. I was dazzled by him, and I felt if the Sinclairs thought he was good enough to be their houseguest, then he must be all right. Only I was wrong."

"You're young," Mrs. Bradford said. "Young girls frequently make mistakes of the heart."

"Quiet, Evelyn," Mr. Bradford said. "Go on, Margaret. How exactly were you wrong?"

Meg could feel them all staring at her. She glanced at Clark, who seemed as interested as the rest of them in her confession. "Nick Sebastian is illegitimate," she said. "That isn't even his name. It's George Keefer. His mother was a tramp, excuse me, Mrs. Bradford, but I don't know how else to describe her. He grew up in squalor, and he lies, he lies about everything. I know now he was only interested in me for my money."

"You have no money," Mr. Bradford pointed out.

"For the money he assumed I must have," Meg said. "Everything you said about him was true, Mr. Bradford. He doesn't belong in Eastgate, with people like us. The Sinclairs know that now, and so do I."

Mr. Bradford nodded. "I only wish you had realized that on Sunday," he said.

"I was a fool," Meg said. "I have no excuse. But I am very sorry."

"William, please," Mrs. Bradford said. "I know you can find it in your heart to forgive Margaret."

"Very well," Mr. Bradford said. "Margaret, I appreciate your apology. You are young, and will outgrow your foolish behavior, I'm sure. There's a recklessness to today's youth that is of great concern to me. My nephew Brad is worrying his mother no end with his choice of companions. Naturally, I want only the best for Clark, and I worry I haven't been selective enough with him. But you are a Winslow, Margaret, no matter who your mother was, and I can see that Grace is doing a fine job raising you. You must be very grateful to her."

"I am," Meg said. "To her and to my uncle Marcus, and all the other people who've shown me so much kindness since my parents died."

"Tragedy, that," Mr. Bradford said. "Well, Grace, why don't you join Evelyn and me for a cup of coffee, and we'll let the young people here have a moment or two to themselves."

"Thank you, William," Aunt Grace said. "I would enjoy that."

Meg couldn't believe she'd pulled it off. She tried to keep from smiling as the adults left the room.

"He's really illegitimate?" Clark asked as soon as they were alone.

"It's not his fault," Meg snapped.

"Then that was all an act," Clark said. "You didn't mean a word you said just now to my father."

"I had to," Meg said. "You don't know the threats Aunt Grace makes."

"She does what she thinks is best for you," Clark said.

"I know what's best for me," Meg said. "Clark, you have to do me a favor."

"What now?" he asked.

"You have to spend Thursday with me," Meg declared. "If your father says it's all right, that is. Ask Aunt Grace if she'll let me see you on Thursday. I'm sure she'll say yes. Then pick me up as early as you can, and we'll tell her we're going to spend the whole day together."

"What do you have planned?" Clark asked.

"I can't tell you," Meg replied. "But believe me, Clark, you're my only chance."

"That's the one thing I do believe," Clark said. "All right, Meg. I'll see what I can do."

Chapter Twelve

It seemed so easy when there were no ladders involved. Clark merely knocked on the door and was admitted by Meg herself. Aunt Grace said a few words of hello and warning (don't go too far, don't come back too late), and then Meg and Clark walked out of the house and entered Clark's car. Meg couldn't get over how simple it was.

"You still want to go through with this?" Clark asked. "You don't have to meet Nick. You can forget all about him, and just spend the day with me."

"I can't forget all about him," Meg replied. "Don't be silly."

Clark laughed. "I'm the one being silly?" he said. "You're risking everything for what, a few hours with someone you hardly know, and you accuse me of being silly?"

"It's not just a few hours," Meg said. "What did Nicky tell you?"

"To pick you up and drop you off and forget I ever saw him," Clark replied. "He made it sound a bit better than that, but basically that was his message."

"I know this is hard for you," Meg declared. "But Nicky and I are doing the right thing. We're both sure of that."

"I hope the right thing doesn't include marriage," Clark said.

Meg was uncertain how to respond. She stared out the window and prayed Nick would be there waiting for her when Clark stopped the car.

"You aren't really planning to elope?" Clark asked. "Meg, I need an honest answer."

"We know what we're doing," Meg said. "We don't have many choices, Clark. Aunt Grace's seen to that."

"If you're so determined to get married, marry me," Clark said. "I mean it, Meg. I can understand why you want to get away from Grace, why you're so scared of the future. I'll marry you today if that's all you want. You may not realize it, but you'd be much happier with me than you ever would be with Nick. I'm like you. We have the same values, we speak a common language."

"I can't marry you," Meg said. "Your father would kill you if we eloped."

"I'll take my chances," Clark replied. "Meg, I love you. You must know that. I've loved you for as long as I can remember. If what you want is to get married, then we'll get married. Just say yes, Meg, and I'll keep on driving until we find a justice of the peace."

"Oh Clark," Meg said. "I do love you. You're the best friend I've ever had. And if all I wanted was to escape, then maybe I would marry you. But it's more than that. What I feel for Nicky is so deep within me. I don't know if I can explain it to you. You say we have the same values, the same language. With Nicky and me, that doesn't matter. Once I met Nicky, I realized that there was a part of me that had always been missing, a part of me that was Nicky. And Nicky realized the same thing about me. Do you understand that? Nicky and I are becoming each other."

"You can't honestly think you'll be happy with him," Clark said. "He has nothing, no family, no money, and if he marries you, no prospects. And you'll have given up everything you have. You're deluding yourself if you think it'll work out."

"You're deluding yourself if you think it won't," Meg declared. "We know what we're giving up to be together. And it's nothing compared to what we're going to have."

Clark kept his eyes on the road, but Meg could see how he clenched the steering wheel and feel his anger. "Are you going to tell me you believe in him?" he asked. "That he hasn't lied to you a hundred times over?"

"Nicky's never lied to me," Meg replied. "Is that all you're worried about, Clark? There wasn't a thing in that detective's report that Nicky hadn't already told me. None of it mattered to me."

"Does he know you don't have any money of your own?" Clark asked. "Did you happen to mention to him just how small your trust fund is, how dependent you are on your aunt and uncle?"

"Stop it, Clark," Meg said. "Just stop it. If you don't want to help, then drop me off right here. I'll get to Nicky without you."

"You don't even know where he is," Clark said. "You're helpless without me."

"I'll take my chances," Meg said.

Clark was silent for a moment, but he kept on driving. "I'll take you," he said. "There are a few things I want to say to Sebastian myself."

"Clark," Meg said.

Clark laughed. "I'm your best friend, remember," he said. "If I can't bless the bride and groom, who can?"

Meg wished the drive would end already, that Clark would vanish and she could be on a bus somewhere with Nick, going toward their future. She never wanted to be parted from him again.

It took another ten minutes before Clark pulled up to a diner. Nick was standing outside, waiting for them, waiting for Meg. He had a suitcase. Meg realized she had nothing, just the clothes she was wearing and seven dollars in her pocketbook. Would Grace let her have the things she'd left behind? Would she ever have the courage to ask for them?

But then, as she got out of the car, and saw Nick smile, it no longer mattered what she'd left behind. She ran to him, and they embraced. Mrs. Nick Sebastian. That was all that mattered.

"Very touching," Clark said. "Glad you could make it, Sebastian."

Nick kept his arm around Meg. "I wish you'd stop calling me that," he said. "Sebastian was my father's name, not mine."

"So I've heard," Clark replied. "Actually, I've heard a lot about you the past few days. I'd be happy to share it with you."

Nick grinned. "My past seems to be endlessly fascinating to you people," he declared. "Grace Winslow couldn't get enough of it, and now you. I don't see why.

It wasn't that much fun to live through. I'd just as soon forget it."

"I'm sure you would," Clark said. "What name are you going to use on the marriage license? George Keefer? Nick Sebastian?"

"I'll use my legal name," Nick said. "Did Daisy tell you we were going to get married?"

"He guessed it," Meg said. "It doesn't matter, Nicky. He won't tell Aunt Grace. And he doesn't know where we're going." She realized she didn't know either, and felt a slight edge of uneasiness.

"I'd like to hear it from you, though," Clark said. "You really plan to marry Meg today?"

"Yes I do," Nick said. "Not that it's any of your business."

Clark took Meg by the arm and pulled her away from Nick. "Listen to me," he demanded. "You know nothing about him, about what kind of man he really is."

"I know him better than I know myself," Meg said.

"You heard my father," Clark said. "He's an animal. He attacked Caroline Sinclair."

Nick laughed. "Caroline Sinclair's idea of an attack is when the man says no," he said. "I never touched her, no matter how much she asked me to."

"I believe Nicky," Meg said.

"I know what's in that report," Clark said. "Your aunt told my father all about it. All he's done is tell lies, lies about his family, his past. Lies about how he got the money for his education."

"He hasn't lied to me," Meg said. "I don't care who else Nicky's lied to. He's been honest with me."

"Meg, please," Clark said. "Come home with me now. You're going to be hurt if you don't."

"Nicky won't hurt me," Meg said. "I know he won't."

"You're right," Clark agreed. "He won't, because he won't have the chance. I'll do the hurting instead."

"What are you talking about?" Meg asked. "You didn't tell anybody what we were doing today? Aunt Grace isn't here, is she?"

"If you did, I'll kill you," Nick said. "Don't you understand what they're threatening her with? Don't you care?"

"Stop it, both of you," Clark said. "I understand, and I care. I care a lot more than you do, Sebastian, or Keefer, or whatever your name is. I wouldn't marry Meg just to sell her back to her family."

"What?" Meg said. "What are you talking about?"

"I'm talking about Nick George," Clark said. "Does that name sound familiar to you, Sebastian?"

"Clark, don't," Nick said.

"Neither one of you has left me any choice," Clark replied. "Meg, I know this is going to hurt you, and I'm sorry. But it's the only way I can think of to make you come to your senses."

"I don't want to hear any lies," Meg said. "Not from you, Clark."

"You've heard enough lies from him," Clark said, nodding his head at Nick. "You know I'll tell you the truth."

"Nicky?" Meg said.

"I love you, Daisy," he said.

"Is that what you said to Elizabeth Stanton?" Clark asked. "I'm sure it must have been."

"Just tell her," Nick said. "That's what you want to do, so do it."

"Tell me what?" Meg asked. "Who's Elizabeth Stanton?"

"She's the sister of a friend of a friend of mine," Clark replied. "She was how old when you pulled this scam on her, seventeen?"

Nick didn't answer. Meg was terrified to look at him, to look at Clark. She stared at the street instead, watching the cars drive by the diner.

"You really are a fool," Clark said to Nick. "I guess someone like you doesn't realize what a small world old money is. The amazing thing is I'm the only one who's found out. Of course you used a different name then, Nick George. But even so, it was a dangerous game to try the same thing twice in so short a time."

"Found out what?" Meg cried. "What's a dangerous game?"

"I'll tell her," Nick said. "Daisy, look at me."

"Don't lie," Clark said. "I know everything that happened, so there's no point lying."

"I don't lie to Daisy," Nick said.

"Sure," Clark said. "You've just forgotten to tell her a few little truths."

Nick stared at Clark with such loathing, it hurt Meg to look at them. "There are a lot of little truths in my life," he said. "Most of them accidents of birth. There's only one big truth, though, and that's my love for Daisy."

"You going to tell her or shall I?" Clark said.

Nick took Meg's hands and made her look straight at him. "I told you I saw my father," he said. "I wanted him to give me money enough for four years' worth of tuition at Princeton. I didn't have a penny to my name. What little I had I'd spent on train fare to North Carolina and a decent suit to see him in. Somehow I thought if I was respectably dressed he'd be more willing to listen to me. I was a fool. I had this fantasy that he'd love me, that he'd say he'd been looking for me all those years. I thought, I've done well in high school, I've supported myself for a year and a half now. I'm smart. I'm not afraid of work. Even if he doesn't love me, even if he feels he can't make me a part of his family, at least he'll be proud. No one had ever been proud of me, Daisy."

"Your mother must have been," Meg said. "Didn't she care you did so well in school?"

Nick shook his head. "It was just one more thing that made my stepfather mad," he replied. "He'd say my grades meant I wasn't working hard enough at home. So one time, in fourth or fifth grade, I flunked everything deliberately, just to see if that would make a difference, but it didn't. He beat me up anyway for being a stupid bum. After that, I figured I might as well get good grades. A beating's a beating, and at least that way my teachers liked me."

"Very touching," Clark said. "But not relevant."

Nick shot Clark an angry look. Meg squeezed Nick's hands. "Go on," she said.

"Sebastian Prescott wasn't proud," Nick said. "I was a fool to think he would be. He said my mother was a whore, that there were any number of men who could have fathered me. He said the thousand dollars he'd paid my mother made her the most expensive lay he'd ever had, but it was worth a few thousand more to him to keep her bastard from bothering him again. Her bastard. Not even his. So he wrote out a check for three thousand and told me to get lost. Are you taking notes, Bradford? Are you writing all this up in your personal report?"

"I'm just trying to understand you," Clark said.

"You can't," Nick said. "But Daisy can, and that's what matters. I took the check and I cashed it right away.

That was shortsighted of me. I should have held on to it, used it for blackmail. But I was too angry, and dammit, I was hurt. I'd had fantasies about him, about how he'd love me. I know I had no right, but he didn't have to be cruel."

"No, he didn't," Meg said.

Nick nodded. "I wanted to hurt back," he said. "I knew he had children, a son and a daughter, and I thought maybe I could get back at him through them, but I couldn't think of a plan. I looked so much like him, I couldn't pretend to be a stranger. If I'd kept the check, I could have shown it to his wife, but all I had was the cash and the resemblance. So I took the next train out of town. I went to New York. I thought, There's no point starting at Princeton, I don't have the money for more than a year. Why bother? So I gave up that goal. Princeton was the only thing I'd ever worked for. I had a teacher once who'd wanted to go to Princeton, but the war got in the way. He said Princeton could make a gentleman out of anybody."

"He was wrong in your case," Clark said.

"Stop it!" Meg said.

"Clark's right," Nick declared. "Not that it matters. I went to New York, and I didn't know what to do. For the first time in my life, I had no plans. I could have gotten scholarship aid for Princeton, God knows I had no money, but I was ashamed of who I was, what I would have had to put down on the application forms. I didn't want people like Clark to know how different I was. And I'd actually counted on Sebastian Prescott paying. I hope I'm never that stupid again."

"So you went looking for someone else to pay," Clark said. "That's where this story is leading."

"First I wasted most of the money," Nick said. "I never had money before, and I wasn't comfortable with his money anyway. So I gambled and I drank and I spent a lot of it on hookers. But then one night one of them said to me that I was so good-looking, she didn't understand why I felt I had to spend money to get a woman to sleep with me. I thought about that a lot after I left, how handsome I was. I went back to my hotel room, and I thought about my assets. I had my looks and roughly a thousand dollars, and brains enough to get into Princeton. It was November, and I knew that the way I'd been spending the money, it would be gone soon, and then I'd have nothing, not even my dreams. So I decided to use my looks and my money and my brains to finance my way through school. I took half the money and bought myself good clothes. Nothing flashy. I went shopping with a hooker I knew. She had excellent taste."

"I'll bet," Clark said.

"Then I decided I'd find a rich girl somewhere and get her to fall in love with me," Nick continued. "I didn't know how it would go from there, but I was sure I'd work something out. I hated everything then, Daisy, the world, myself, everything. I didn't care if I hurt people."

"That's because you were hurt," Meg said.

"You're not feeling sorry for him," Clark said.

"She probably is," Nick declared. "I can make people do that, pity me. It's one of my talents. I used it then. I made up a story about who I was. It wasn't the truth, and it wasn't the story I tell people at Princeton. I said I was Nick George, and my mother had come from a good family in Seattle, only she'd been disinherited when she'd married my father. Religious differences. They'd been poor but oh so happy until one day my father was killed by a hit-and-run driver. I was seven. I saw him die. I liked that part and told it really well. Elizabeth cried when I described it to her. My mother worked hard to support the two of us. She saw to it that I had all the best things, a good education, riding lessons. It was important to her that I assume my rightful place in society. So when I was sixteen, she took me back to Seattle for her parents to meet. Only they wouldn't even see us. Doors slammed in our faces, things like that. It broke my mother's heart. She died six months later, and I was left on my own. One of my teachers took me in, but I knew I couldn't be dependent on his charity forever, and besides, I had ambitions. I wanted to show my mother's family that they'd made a mistake rejecting me. I'd get this quiver in my voice when I reached that part, so she could see that underneath my defiance was pain. Girls like that, Clark. You're naturally pathetic yourself, so you should do well."

"Why did you lie to her, Nicky?" Meg asked. "She would have loved you if you told her the truth."

"Oh Daisy," Nick said. "Just because you love me doesn't mean anybody else would. Besides, I didn't want her to love who I really was. All I wanted was her family's money."

"How did you meet her?" Clark asked.

"I crashed a New Year's party at her country club," Nick said. "It didn't matter who she was. I picked Elizabeth because she wasn't pretty and nobody danced with her twice. Rich girls always seem to have someone to dance with, but the ones who aren't pretty don't get repeats. We danced five times. I told her lies, and made a date with her for the following day, and when I saw her next I told her that everything I'd said the night before had been lies, that the truth was Seattle and disinheritance and hit-and-run driver and rejection. I said I could tell she came from a good family and I'd understand if she never wanted to see me again, that I wasn't worthy of her. She said I was the bravest boy she'd ever met."

"Did you tell her you loved her?" Clark asked.

"Not then," Nick said. "Not for another two weeks. She was a senior in high school and she lived with her parents. At first we dated openly, but when her parents started to ask questions, I convinced Elizabeth we had to see each other on the sly. She liked that, and I did too. I didn't have much money left, and she expected to be taken out to expensive restaurants. Our secret dates cost a lot less money."

"Nicky, don't," Meg said.

"I have to," he said. "You have to know. I should have told you right away, but I thought I could get away with it. Clark's right. I have been lying to you. You're not Elizabeth. You deserve the truth."

Meg nodded. The sun came out from behind a cloud and forced her to squint as she looked up at Nick.

"The rest went pretty easily," Nick said. "I convinced Elizabeth that her parents would force us to part unless we got married. She was all in favor. We eloped. It was easy enough to keep from consummating the union. She was too scared, and I sure didn't want to. So I took her home. Her father asked me what my price was for a no-publicity annulment. I said twenty thousand. We went to the bank, and he gave me a cashier's check. Then we went to his lawyer, and I signed lots of papers Nick George. He saw me to the train station. The whole thing took five weeks. I reapplied to Princeton, bought a new wardrobe, and changed my name legally to Nicholas George Sebastian. I knew I wasn't entitled to the name Prescott, but after what I'd done to the Stantons, I felt I could claim at least part of my father's name. In September, I started Princeton. In July, I met you. Did I leave any pertinent details out, Clark? I think I covered pretty much everything."

"I didn't want you to know, Meg," Clark said. "I found out this week, after you told me Nick's real name. It rang a bell. Then I remembered a friend of mine had told me a story about someone he knew, whose kid sister had fallen in love with some drifter and her parents had paid a lot of money to break them up. Nick George, he'd said the guy was named. We'd been talking about people whose last names could also be first names, like me, Clark Bradford. Nick George. Nicholas George Keefer. I'd never trusted him, so I called my friend, and he called his, and we exchanged descriptions, and I knew it had to be the same guy. I wanted to protect you, Meg. I wanted to keep you from knowing. But I couldn't think of any other way of stopping you. I'm sorry. I know you must hate me. I only hope you hate him too."

Meg covered her eyes with her hands. The sun was giving her a headache. She didn't know what she felt.

"You'd better leave," Clark said to Nick. "Forget about Eastgate and Meg, and Princeton, for that matter. Take your scams someplace else. Create a pathetic new identity for yourself."

"I don't deny I've created myself," Nick replied. "I never saw that I had any other choice. Not until now, not until Daisy."

"Leave her alone," Clark said. "Come on, Meg, I'll take you home."

"No!" Meg said. "No. Stop it."

"I'll do whatever you want, Daisy," Nick said. "Just tell me what to do."

Meg realized then what a difficult thing it was to be a liar, and what an enormous thing it was to love one. Liars lied and were lied about, and knowing all those lies, found it hard to trust in others. To love a liar meant you had to believe in him, in spite of his lies and the lies told about him, in spite of his inability to trust. She knew that simply by loving Nick, she had become a liar, that just as she had taught him right from wrong, he had taught her the value of untruth.

"Let's do it," she said in a hard, flat voice. "Let's elope anyway, and Clark will tell Aunt Grace where we are, and she'll pay you a lot of money, the way the Stantons did."

"Meg!" Clark said.

Meg shook her head. "It's the best plan," she said. "That way Nicky will have money, more than enough, and he'll still have me. We'll get married anyway, on my eighteenth birthday. He can use the money Aunt Grace gives him to rescue me. She won't know it, but it'll be her wedding present to us. All right, Nicky? We can take the next bus out of town. The less head start we have on Clark, the easier it'll be for Aunt Grace to find us."

"No," Nick said.

"Why not?" Meg demanded. "You said you'd do whatever I wanted. Well, this is what I want."

"I thought I could," Nick said. "I wish I could. George Keefer could. He wouldn't care what became of you. I thought for you I could do anything, but I can't. I can't become George Keefer again. Not even for you, Daisy. I'm sorry."

"Come on, Meg," Clark said. "I'll take you home. Grace doesn't have to know any of this ever happened."

Nick shook his head. "I'll take her back to Grace's," he said. "Thank you, Clark, but you've done enough. From now on, Daisy and I will handle things on our own."

CHAPTER THIRTEEN

The cab dropped them off in front of Aunt Grace's cottage. Meg hated the idea of going back into the house, and walked away from it instead. Nick followed her, suitcase in hand, until she finally stopped at the gazebo.

"Talk to me," he said. "I have to know how you feel."

"I feel cheated," Meg replied. She sat down on the wrought-iron love seat. Nick put his suitcase down and sat beside her. "I don't see why we didn't elope. If we get caught, fine, you just end up with money. If we don't get caught, even better. Why did you bring me back here?"

"Because I'm selfish," Nick replied.

Meg looked into Nick's eyes. "I know you love me," she said. "I know this was never a scam for you."

Nick smiled. "Never," he agreed. "Things would have been a lot easier if it had been."

"Then what's the problem?" Meg asked. "We'll

never have another chance like today. Clark will see to that."

"Daisy, listen to me," Nick said. "Listen to me and forgive me. Everything Clark said today was true. All the things he didn't say were true also. He sees me as a corrupter, someone destroying all that's moral and true about you. Did you look at him when you said we should elope for the money? He was stricken."

"What do I care how Clark feels," Meg said. "Or Aunt Grace or Uncle Marcus or the entire population of Eastgate and Boston combined. All I care about is you. What you're willing to do, I'm willing to do."

Nick shook his head. "I'm not willing anymore," he said. "Blame it on Princeton, blame it on yourself. When I went after Elizabeth, I was angry and I was scared. At Princeton, I lost some of that anger and a little of the fear. Since I've met you, the fear and the anger are gone completely. I'm not sure yet what's replacing them; I don't have words in my vocabulary for what I feel. But I don't want to hurt people just to get what I need. I don't feel justified in doing it anymore."

"Did you hurt Elizabeth?" Meg asked. She didn't even like mentioning the other girl's name.

"I must have," Nick said. "I didn't stick around long enough to find out, though. I've hurt you just by having done that to Elizabeth. I didn't want you to know. I'm ashamed of a lot of things in my life, but Elizabeth is different. Elizabeth I feel guilty about."

"Not guilty enough to return the money," Meg said.

"Do you want me to?" Nick asked. "I will if you want me to."

"No," Meg said. "I want you to have Princeton. I'm starting to understand how important it is for you."

"For a long time, it was the only thing I had," Nick said. "Now I have you."

"But Princeton is still important," Meg said.

Nick nodded. Meg smiled at him.

"We'll have sons," she said. "Thousands of them. And we'll send them all to Princeton."

"One girl," he said. "Who'll look exactly like you."

"If you insist," Meg said. "Nicky, I have to have that. I have to know we're going to be together."

"We will be," Nick said. "But honestly. Through the front door. No sneaking around."

"On my eighteenth birthday," Meg said, and then she took a deep breath, and made a sacrifice for love. "No, on my nineteenth. We'll wait the extra year so you can get your degree first."

"I love you," Nick said, and he kissed her to prove it.

Meg smiled at him. "There's something I want to do," she said. "We talked about it. Burning your name, your past."

"Are you sure?" Nick asked.

"Positive," she replied. "Stay there. I'm going to burn all sorts of awful things." She gave him a kiss, then ran to the cottage, and went up to her bedroom. She wanted only the best symbols of their previous unhappiness to destroy. The copy of the detective's report Aunt Grace had given her was an obvious pick. But there had to be something else, something she could contribute. And then she found the pink ruffled party dress.

Meg whooped with pleasure, grabbed the dress from its hanger, then went to the kitchen and took some matches. The house was empty, and she wasn't scared. It was a wonderful feeling to be in that house and not feel dread.

Nick was waiting at the gazebo for her. "The dress?" he asked. "I met you in that dress."

Meg ripped off a ruffle for him. "Sleep with it under your pillow," she said. "The rest is ashes."

Nick laughed, but there was no echo of anger. "What's that?" he asked.

"The detective's report," Meg said. "How's that for cheap and easy symbolism."

"Perfect," he said. "Is it safe to build a fire here?"

"Probably not," Meg said. They stood outside the gazebo as Meg ripped up the report, then piled the dress on top of it. "I consign our past to ashes!" she cried, and struck a match. The flame caught, and she started burning the paper. Soon the dress had caught fire as well. Meg watched the smoke billow up, and felt light and happy, the way she had as a little girl. She could see the joy on Nick's face as well. They had no more past, just future, blissful, perfect future.

"*Margaret Louise Winslow!*"

Meg turned around and saw Aunt Grace marching toward them. There was no place to hide Nick, no way to protect either of them from Grace's wrath. She started to run, but Nick held her back, put his arm around her, and stood his ground.

"What is the meaning of this?" Aunt Grace shouted. "Setting fires on the property. Seeing this man. Disobeying my orders. Have you truly lost all your senses?"

Meg felt Nick's warmth enveloping her. The fire kept burning. They had no past, just future. "No, Aunt Grace," she said. "I haven't lost any of my senses."

"Go to your room at once!" Aunt Grace said. "Mr. Sebastian, if you don't leave immediately, I shall have to call the police."

"Call them," Nick said.

Aunt Grace stared down at the fire, and stamped on it to put the flames out. "Your dress!" she cried. "You're burning the dress I bought you."

"I hate that dress," Meg said. She had never been honest before with Aunt Grace. It was a dizzying sensation.

"But it was so pretty," Aunt Grace said, and for just a moment, Meg could see that her aunt was a human being too. "I always wanted a dress like that, but my mother wouldn't let me have one. She said girls my size should never wear ruffles. So I bought one for you."

"Oh Aunt Grace," Meg said. "I'm sorry. Why didn't you ever tell me?"

"I don't know," she said. "I didn't think it mattered."

Meg wasn't sure, but she suspected it did. She left Nick's side, walked over to Grace, and embraced her.

The gesture returned Aunt Grace to her normal awful self. "You have a great deal of explaining to do," she said, brushing Meg away. "Would you prefer to do it here or at the sanitarium?"

"Stop with the sanitarium already," Nick said. "Stop frightening Daisy. You gain nothing from it, and you're only hurting her."

"I know what's best for my niece," Aunt Grace declared.

"No you don't," he said. "You thought pink ruffles were what's best. You thought locking her up was what's best. You thought keeping us apart was what's best. You were wrong on all three counts."

"I am Margaret's legal guardian," Aunt Grace said. "As such, I can control her future for at least the next two years. I suggest you respect that power, Mr. Sebastian, and not provoke me into punishing Margaret even further."

"If you do one more thing to Daisy, you'll have me to answer to," Nick said.

"Stop it!" Meg said. "Both of you, just stop it."

It was a tone neither of them had ever heard her use before, and it shocked them both.

"You're being foolish," Meg declared. "Both of you." She marveled at her courage.

"Margaret," Aunt Grace said as Nick was saying, "Daisy."

"Nobody's going to hurt anybody," Meg said. "Not anymore. And we're not going to shout at each other either. We're going to sit right here in this gazebo and talk like three rational human beings. Do you think the two of you can manage that?"

Nick laughed. "It'll be a stretch," he said. "But I'll try."

"I don't care for this tone at all," Aunt Grace said, but she entered the gazebo with them.

"I haven't been honest with you, Aunt Grace," Meg said. "You forbade me to see Nicky, and I've been seeing him anyway."

"You will have to be punished," Aunt Grace replied. "I'm afraid when I tell Marcus what you've been doing, he'll insist on something quite severe."

"It doesn't matter," Meg said. "You can do whatever you like with me, and I'll still love Nicky."

"I'm sure you will," Aunt Grace said. "But will he still love you?"

Nick nodded. "Forever, I'm afraid."

Aunt Grace turned to him. "Perhaps I've been focusing on the wrong person," she said. "Perhaps the best form of punishment for Margaret is to punish you."

"How?" Nick asked. "I haven't committed any crimes. And I doubt you're going to lock me up in your house."

"I can give a copy of the detective's report to the Sinclair family," Aunt Grace declared. "Robert Sinclair can read it, then tell all his cronies at Princeton the truth about your parentage. You'll have no friends there once they learn how you've been lying to them."

"Aunt Grace," Meg said. "Don't hurt Nicky. It isn't fair."

"She won't be hurting me," Nick said. "Feel free to tell the world what you've learned, Miss Winslow," he declared. "Three months ago, it would have mattered to me. Now it doesn't. Daisy's the only one who counts, and she knows everything."

"I'm sure if I had to, I could have you expelled from Princeton," Aunt Grace said. "They must have some sort of moral code there, and I undoubtedly number enough Princeton alumni among my friends to see it enforced."

"Miss Winslow, I'm going to marry Daisy," Nick said. "We'll all be better off if that's a given in this conversation. Now, I can marry her today, or tomorrow, or two years from now, but one way or another, we're going to be married. I imagine I'll seem a little less awful to you if I've graduated from Princeton, but if that's truly unimportant to you, then get me expelled. The sooner I'm out of Princeton, the sooner I'll marry Daisy."

"You won't be able to marry her if she's locked away in a sanitarium," Aunt Grace threatened. "I have the power to do that."

"But you don't want to," Nick said. "It's taken me a while to figure that out. It's a hollow threat."

"Perhaps it was before," Grace said. "But you're forcing me to consider it seriously."

Nick shook his head. "The only way you can do it is by telling Marcus everything," he said. "And that would include the fact that Daisy and I were going to elope today. See my suitcase, all nicely packed. We had our bus picked out, our plans all made. You don't want Marcus to know that. You don't want him to think you incompetent. You have your pride too, Miss Winslow."

Aunt Grace stared at Nick. "I am never going to like you," she declared.

Nick smiled back at her. "Nor I you," he said.

"But I love both of you," Meg said. "Aunt Grace, I know, deep down, that you've only been doing what you think is best for me. It's not always easy to love people. I believe that both of you love me. That gives me a few rights."

"Rights?" Aunt Grace said.

"Yes, rights," Meg said. "Like the right to tell the truth. Nicky and I were going to elope today, Aunt Grace. I'd already met him. We came back here because he changed his mind. He didn't want us to get married behind your back. He wanted us to be aboveboard about it. I was the one pushing for the elopement. If I'd had my way, you never would have seen me again."

"Am I supposed to be grateful to Mr. Sebastian, then?" Aunt Grace asked.

"Yes," Meg replied. "You are."

Aunt Grace laughed.

"I don't expect your gratitude," Nick said. "Daisy doesn't either, not really. But we'd both appreciate a little understanding on your part. If Daisy feels you love her, then I'm willing to concede that you do. And if you do, then you want what's best for her."

"Which hardly includes you," Aunt Grace declared.

"You may be right about that," Nick said. "I admit I'm being selfish. But so are you."

"How?" Aunt Grace asked. "I have made innumerable sacrifices for that girl."

"I have too," Nick said. "She's worth them, don't you think?"

For one blessed moment, Aunt Grace was silent. She looked first at Meg, then at Nick. "How much?" she asked. "What's your price?"

"Let Daisy finish her education at Miss Arnold's," Nick said. "No more talk about sanitariums, and expensive British reform schools. She has two years to go, let her spend them at the only home she knows."

"And what do you give up?" Aunt Grace asked.

"We won't get married until I graduate Princeton," Nick said. "That's three years from now. You can spend those three years throwing proper suitors Daisy's way. You can spend them making mischief for me. In the meantime, Daisy will graduate and make her debut. Maybe she'll fall out of love with me. You can certainly hope so."

"There must be no talk of engagement," Aunt Grace declared. "No rings, no tokens of affection. Margaret must be free to move around in her proper sphere, to meet the right sort of young man."

"No engagement," Nick said. "Not until her debut."

"Not until a full year after her debut," Aunt Grace said. "Any engagement will be contingent upon your graduation from Princeton."

"Fair enough," Nick said.

"And you are not to see each other again until Margaret turns eighteen," Aunt Grace said.

"Aunt Grace!" Meg cried.

"I am being very generous to you, Margaret. Consider the alternatives to two years at Miss Arnold's."

"She's right," Nick said. "No matter what they do to you, we won't be able to see each other. At least at Miss Arnold's, you'll be less unhappy."

Meg stared out at the ocean. To love a liar meant to be a liar. "All right," she said. "But you have to let us write letters."

"No letters," Aunt Grace said. "No phone calls or secret messages either."

Meg shook her head. "No letters, no deal," she said. "I'll run away if I have to. And I'll tell the newspapers everything. How you kept me locked up, and threatened to put me away in a sanitarium, just because I loved an impoverished college student. You'll love that, Aunt Grace, the reporters hanging around, demanding to see where I was held prisoner. I can play pathetic heiress if I have to."

"You may write letters," Aunt Grace said. "Judging from the letters I've received from you, Margaret, their tedious nature should put a swift end to your relationship. And I doubt Mr. Sebastian's grunts of passion will maintain their appeal on paper."

Meg smiled. Her triumphs over Aunt Grace had been few. That made this one even sweeter.

"I have one final condition, however," Aunt Grace said. "Should the three years pass, and the two of you wed anyway, you are both to know that I will cut Margaret out of my will completely."

"So what?" Nick asked.

"So she will be a pauper," Aunt Grace said. "All she will have is the interest she receives from her trust fund, which currently comes to less than four thousand a year.

My estate is worth millions. That is what Margaret will be giving up in exchange for you, Mr. Sebastian. That is what you'll be losing if you marry her instead of some nouveau riche creature whose family will be charmed by your smile and your lies. And don't expect my heart to soften as years go by. There will be no change in my will."

"I'd never expect your heart to soften," Nick said. "And frankly, I wouldn't want any of your money anyway. The older I get, the more distasteful I find handouts. But if it's important to Daisy, then she can dump me."

Meg laughed.

"Then that's settled," Nick said. "We don't see each other for two years, no engagement or marriage for three. Daisy gets to finish school at Miss Arnold's, and you can't threaten to send her someplace else. She makes her debut, dates as many fellows as you can round up for her. We don't speak to each other on the phone, but we do get to write letters. At the end of all of which, when we marry, she's out of your will. I assume she was never in Marcus's."

"You assume correctly," Aunt Grace replied. "If I find that you have violated any of the terms of this agreement, then Margaret will be sent to St. Bartholomew's."

"No," Nick said. "No more threats like that hanging over her head."

"Then I'll see to it that you're expelled from Princeton," Aunt Grace declared. "Is that acceptable?"

Nick nodded.

"Very well," Aunt Grace said. "The agreement is effective immediately. Come, Margaret, back to the house. Mr. Sebastian, I suggest that you take your suitcase and leave Eastgate immediately. If I find out that you and

Margaret have seen each other again before the summer ends, then I will be forced to send Margaret away, someplace you won't be able to find her. And that is not a hollow threat."

"You have to let us say good-bye," Meg said. "We aren't going to see each other again for two years, you can at least give us five minutes."

"I don't have to do anything," Aunt Grace said. "But I suppose five minutes is a small price to pay to keep you from sulking all summer. I shall be standing right outside the gazebo. When the five minutes are up, I'll let you know." She got up, stared at Nick and Meg, then left them alone.

"Five minutes," Meg said. "Two years."

Nick shook his head. "Come here," he said, and Meg did. They held each other for a long moment, then kissed for an even longer one. "This is the right thing," he said. "It's worth losing this summer to keep you from harm."

"I'll write to you every day," Meg said.

"You'd better not," Nick replied. "She'll change the rules on us if you push her too hard. A letter a week, and if she makes noises, we'll cut down."

"I love you," Meg said. "I love you so much."

Nick nodded. "I love you too," he said. "We are so lucky. I can't get over it, how lucky we are."

"I don't feel lucky," Meg said.

"Oh Daisy," Nick said, and he kissed her again. "It's just three years. The same three years we'd agreed on ourselves. And this way, at least we have letters, and the promise of what's to come."

"I won't be able to live without seeing you," Meg said. "Not for two years."

"We'll see each other," Nick whispered. "Somehow, somewhere. She won't know."

Meg smiled at him. "I love you, Nicky," she said. "Now and forever. I'll love you until the day we die."

Nick put his fingers on her mouth to shush her. "Don't say that," he murmured. "There's no need to. Don't you know? We're never going to die."

CHAPTER FOURTEEN

The doorbell rang. "I'll get it," Evvie said. "It's probably Sam."

And it was. "Twin delivery," he said, wheeling the babies in. "Where do you want them?"

"The floor will do," Evvie replied. Sam unstrapped the babies, and soon they were crawling in opposite directions. Rob paddled his way toward the kitchen, while Mickey began tugging at Claire's calf. Claire laughed, and picked him up.

"A real ladies' man, I see," she said. "You know, he looks like Nicky."

"Megs thinks so," Evvie said.

Thea scooped Rob up off the floor. "He looks healthy enough," she admitted. "Although I still say you weaned them too soon."

"Not again," Sybil said. "I can't take another breast-feeding war."

"Where's Megs?" Sam asked. "I'd have thought she'd be down here visiting with you."

"She's in the attic," Evvie replied. "Reading Nicky's old love letters, I think."

"She's sorting things out," Thea said. "She wanted some time alone before the wedding tomorrow."

"She'd better hurry, then," Sam said. "Clark called me right before I left. He's planning to pick Megs up at six."

"When's Duncan getting there?" Claire asked as Mickey contentedly yanked at her hair.

"Closer to seven," Sam said. "He wanted to finish everything at the office, so he could go on his honeymoon with a clear conscience."

Claire laughed. "Not the sort of thing Nicky ever worried about," she said.

"I wonder how Megs is going to like being married to a doctor," Thea said. "It's going to be so different from what she's used to."

"Duncan's a good man," Sam declared. "And he's crazy about Megs. I think they'll be very happy together."

"Sam's such a romantic," Evvie said.

"I'm predisposed to like doctors," Sam replied. "My grandfather was one. My sister-in-law is one. Besides, if Megs marries Duncan, it means she won't marry Clark. Which cuts down considerably on the amount of time I'd have to spend with Schyler."

"What if I marry Schyler?" Claire asked. "There's more than one way to get him into the family."

"He already is in our family," Sybil said. "He's our half cousin, remember."

"He's a half-wit, you mean," Sam said.

Evvie laughed. "Sam hates people who are twenty times better-looking than he is. Fortunately for me, I'm only ten times."

"Clark's going to be here in half an hour," Thea said.

"Don't you think we should make Megs get a move on? She'll need a shower after all that time in the attic."

"I'll go," Claire said. "Here, Sam, take your first-born." She handed Mickey over to him.

"I'll go with you," Sybil declared.

"Are you sure?" Claire asked.

Sybil nodded. "I can manage the stairs," she replied. She grabbed her cane, and walked out of the parlor with Claire.

Thea shook her head. "I wouldn't have dared ask," she said. "Sybil bites my head off if I mention her legs."

"She's that way with us too," Evvie said. "Claire's the only one who can really talk to her."

"It works out well," Sam said. "Sybil's the only one who can really talk to Claire." He frowned. "Do you think Claire's serious about marrying Schyler?" he asked.

Evvie laughed. "Just tell Claire it's what Nicky would have wanted," she said. "That'll stop her cold."

"Is this what Nicky would have wanted?" Thea asked. "Megs remarrying?"

"I think so," Sam said. "I really think he would have been happy. He spent a lot of his life looking out for Megs. He wouldn't have wanted her to be unprotected."

Evvie smiled. "I love you," she said to her husband. "Come on, let's change the babies before Clark gets here."

"I'll help," Thea said. "I am a professional, you know."

Claire and Sybil climbed the back staircase, which led to the attic door.

When Claire opened the door and looked up, they could see Megs was propped against an old chair, letters in her hand. Her eyes were closed, and her breathing deep, but the expression on her face was peaceful, and she was smiling.

Claire stared at the furniture and the boxes and the dust. "What a dump," she whispered. "Should I go up there to wake her?"

Sybil shook her head. "Leave her alone," she said. "She only looks that way when she's dreaming of Nicky."

ABOUT THE AUTHOR

SUSAN BETH PFEFFER graduated from New York University with a degree in television, motion pictures, and radio studies. She is the author of the highly praised *The Year Without Michael*, which was an ALA Best Book for Young Adults and a *Publishers Weekly*'s Best Book of the Year, and many other acclaimed young adult novels, including *About David*, *Fantasy Summer*, *Getting Even*, and *Evvie at Sixteen*, *Thea at Sixteen*, *Claire at Sixteen*, and *Sybil at Sixteen*, the first four books in The Sebastian Sisters quintet. Susan Beth Pfeffer is a native New Yorker who currently resides in Middletown, New York.

ABOUT THE AUTHOR

SUSAN [illegible] graduated from New York University [illegible] a figure in [illegible] [illegible] and radio stations. She is the author of [illegible] The [illegible] [illegible], which won [illegible] Best Book for Young People and a Publishers Weekly Best Book of the Year, and many [illegible] acclaimed young adult novels, including [illegible] [illegible], Getting [illegible], and [illegible] [illegible] [illegible] [illegible] [illegible] [illegible] and [illegible] [illegible] [illegible] books [illegible] The [illegible] [illegible] [illegible] [illegible] a native New Yorker who [illegible] resides in [illegible], New York.

THE SEBASTIAN SISTERS

Susan Beth Pfeffer

An compelling series that follows the fortunes of four sisters – Evvie, Thea, Claire and Sybil – as each reaches the landmark of a sixteenth birthday and must face up to new challenges and relationships.

'Fairly sparkles with romance . . . the Sebastians have established themselves as a family to watch' PUBLISHERS WEEKLY

Available now:

1. EVVIE AT SIXTEEN	0 553 401459
2. THEA AT SIXTEEN	0 553 401567
3. CLAIRE AT SIXTEEN	0 553 401475
4. SYBIL AT SIXTEEN	0 553 401483
5. MEG AT SIXTEEN	0 553 401491